The Little Book of Goodbyes

RAVI SHANKAR ETTETH is a writer, editor, graphic designer and political cartoonist. In a career spanning forty years, he has worked with and headed editorial at some of the biggest media groups in the country, among them the *New Indian Express*, the *Sunday Standard*, *India Today*, *Media Transasia*, the Observer Group, while launching six news channels and a lifestyle channel on television. He is the author of several bestselling and critically acclaimed novels including *The Tiger by the River*, *The Scream of the Dragonflies*, *The Brahmin* and *The Return of the Brahmin*.

The Little Book of Goodbyes

Ravi Shankar Etteth

Published by Westland Books, a division of Nasadiya Technologies Private Limited, in 2025

No. 269/2B, First Floor, 'Irai Arul', Vimalraj Street, Nethaji Nagar, Alapakkam Main Road, Maduravoyal, Chennai 600095

Westland and the Westland logo are the trademarks of Nasadiya Technologies Private Limited, or its affiliates.

Copyright © Ravi Shankar Etteth, 2025

Ravi Shankar Etteth asserts the moral right to be identified as the author of this work.

ISBN: 9789371975353

10 9 8 7 6 5 4 3 2 1

This is a work of fiction. Names, characters, organisations, places, events and incidents are either products of the author's imagination or used fictitiously.

All rights reserved

Typeset by Jojy Philip

Printed at Replika Press Pvt. Ltd

No part of this book may be reproduced, or stored in a retrieval system, or transmitted in any form or by any means, electronic, mechanical, photocopying, recording, or otherwise, without express written permission of the publisher.

For Shampa,
the wave, the rock

To Begin With

Love is difficult to trust. A few months after the pandemic ended, a cop friend of mine told me he was investigating the suicide of a couple in their thirties. They had abandoned their ageing parents who had contracted the virus. Their suicide note confessed they couldn't take the guilt any more.

Surviving the pandemic made me think about things people take for granted, or are inevitable, such as love, loss and fear at a time when people were dropping like flies in summer. Now that the virus has become like any other flu, I wonder whether those who fled in panic can face themselves every day without flinching? Was saving oneself worth the guilt? Prayers won't ward off the ghosts because these survivors are already haunted. They will always be.

The last time I saw my father was on the screen of a friend's cell phone with a weak connection. He was ninety-two when he died in Palakkad 3,000 kilometres away from my house in Lansdowne where I was holed up, away from the virus that stalked Delhi's streets. Because of the lockdown I couldn't go back home to conduct the last rites. My brother, who was my father's primary caregiver, cremated him. My final sight of my father, with whom I had a complicated relationship, was of his aristocratic nose and heavy eyelids that had closed for the last time, framed in a white cotton shroud. Do I feel guilty? No. Travel was beyond my control. Do I regret not going? Yes, and always will. Because I cannot now ask his forgiveness for not being there and for not being the son I was supposed to be. That still hurts.

In 1998, my mother and I fought the good fight together in the ICU of a Kochi hospital with pep talks, jokes and faith.

'You'll be all right,' I told her, daring to trust myself.

'You think so?' she asked, desperately wanting to believe me. We fought death with blood transfusions, plasma bags and entreaties to the doctors and the gods. I did not acknowledge to myself that the fight was already lost. I walked to the ICU and saw my dead mother from the corner of my left eye, and couldn't bring myself to look at her. I still find it hard to turn my head to the left, because then, I will see her. Dead. I will say goodbye to her one day, if someone helps me look left at last.

The first dead person I saw was my grandfather. He was borne away on a sunlit road that meandered its way through a vast carpet of paddy-fringed woods where I, as a child, had accompanied him on his hunting forays.

All this morbid talk doesn't mean all farewells are painful. Sure, I have lost friends. Said goodbye to a wife, children, partners, lovers, pets. I have ghosted girlfriends and floated away from friends. I have lost jobs. Art has been stolen. Clothes and jewellery have been purloined. I even lost a favourite pair of shades at an airport. I was too busy with my priorities, impatient to want something better; I never attempted to feel what others felt.

The other day, at a party, I met a recovering addict. I had a slight cold, and snorted involuntarily. 'Please don't do that,' he begged me. He hadn't yet let addiction go, because it meant admitting to himself that he was happiest when high. But he had the good sense to stay the course because he knew it would kill him otherwise.

There are bad things that surprisingly make us happy. There are good things that make us unhappy. How we feel about what happens around us and how we react defines us. There is good in bad men, and some bad in good men. I don't know what I am. But my advice would be to say goodbye to everything that diminishes you, and binds you to the passions of others. A goodbye is not always about grief or regret. It is also love. Like the Adamsons letting their lion cub Elsa free to go back to the savannah and join her kind.

The French are wrong. When you say goodbye, a part of you doesn't die. It changes into something stronger.

New Delhi
27 July 2025

KERALA
OLD & NEW

The Gene That Guards Us

This is the story of a man, his dog Fang, and a gene that travelled a million years to the twentieth century from the Great Ice Age. It was the 1920s. My grandfather was commanding a battalion of the MSP—short for Malabar Special Police—which was tasked with putting down the Moplah insurrection in Kerala. It was a job they did admirably well. The Moplahs were Muslim farmers who revolted against British authority for taking away their agricultural rights; much pillaging, pogroms and forcible conversions to Islam took place during the violence that lasted about six months. The beleaguered British modernised the MSP; my grandfather was one of the commandants in charge of northern Kerala where the killing was the worst. Having fought the Germans in the First World War, he considered fighting angry peasants no big deal. However, he would take his men on long route marches, sometimes a distance of twenty miles both ways, to keep them in shape. Some of them would grumble, but the sight of Fang walking ahead in step with their commanding officer silenced them.

Fang's arrival in the MSP camp almost killed him. One night, my grandfather was woken by a low keening coming from under his bed. He barked at the sentry who rushed in with a lantern, 'What are you waiting for, man? If it's a Moplah, shoot him.'

The sentry shone his lantern under the bed, straightened up and saluted. 'I can't sir, it's a pup.'

A half-grown pup cowered under the bed. 'Come 'ere, boy,' my grandfather held out his hand, ignoring the fact that the sentry had disobeyed a direct order, which in other circumstances would have led to his dismissal. Because Grandfather understood that his men who would shoot rebels without a thought wouldn't hurt a wounded pup.

The pup slowly crawled forward and licked the outstretched hand, all the while looking steadily at Grandfather with unblinking yellow eyes. Its sides were streaked with blood, furrowed, having crawled through the barbed wire.

'We don't have a vet, call the doctor!' Grandfather ordered.

The doctor, protesting that he was not a vet, sedated the pup, gave it antibiotic shots and put iodine on the cuts. Every Tuesday and Saturday, the soldiers held prayers at the camp temple for the animal's survival. One night, Grandfather was woken up by something sloshing all over his face. The pup was licking his face. My grandfather named him Fang.

A self-taught man, his favourite author was Jack London, and *White Fang* his favourite book. A photograph of Fang as the camp mascot now hangs in my study, with the dog sitting at the feet of my grandfather, fitted out in full uniform, medals and all. Fang looked different from other dogs, with furry ears and a black snout. 'It's a wolf dog,' a friend remarked.

Then I knew how Fang had got his name.

Jack London's White Fang is a fierce wolf dog who saves his owner Scott's father's life from a killer, and almost gets killed himself. I've often wondered if Grandfather's Fang carried the gene of a wolf which was domesticated one million years ago by some prehistoric man who wanted a bit of companionship during his long journeys through primordial forests. Fang went on to lead a long and happy life, and went on many route marches, always ahead of the men. Until, one night, a rebel snuck into Grandfather's tent with a knife when he was asleep. Fang leaped up from his corner and went for the intruder's throat. The man tried to shake the dog off while trying to stab Grandfather. The knife went through Fang. Grandfather, now awake, shot the man. But the dog was dead, his jaws still clamped on the trespasser's throat. The camp held a full military farewell for Fang, gun salutes and all, while he lay in state, draped in the battalion flag.

A farewell was said. A debt was repaid.

My grandfather insisted that the two Fangs—Jack London's and his—were the same, separated by time. It was absolute bosh, of course, except for the fact that all belief is flawed without faith.

After I heard about Fang, I wanted a Fang of my own. I had faith that I would get mine some day. I have kept many dogs but there was always something missing. Until I found Bosky, a Labrador Retriever cross with a silky mane, seductive eyes with long golden lashes, and the widest smile god ever gave a dog. She would be with me always; on walks, drives, while I read a book, watched telly, drank with buddies, slept on the sofa in my bedroom at night. One of our favourite activities was going for after-dinner walks in the neighbourhood. It was a quiet place then, with little traffic at night, except for the random motorcycle or car speeding along the road that skirted a huge park housing the ruins of a Mughal palace. On a full-moon night, we would often hear the foxes howling in the woods and the night-birds singing in the trees gilded silver with moonlight. Bosky might stop and peer across the shining grass into the thick copse where the shadows hid from the moon, where perhaps the ghosts of Mughal gentlemen collected for a phantom hunt. Emboldened by her at my side, I often wished I could go ghost-hunting, or at least fox-spotting.

One night, I gathered up my courage. Whistling for Bosky, I sprinted across the road and was suddenly flung forward by a heavy force. I found myself lying on the sidewalk with Bosky on top of me. There was a screech of tyres and a car sped away without headlights; had they been switched on, I would have waited for it to pass. Dazed, I struggled to sit up—I was lying face down—with Bosky, unmoving, on top of me. I realised she had leaped on me to push me away and had been hit by the speeding car. I placed her in the backseat of my car and drove to the vet as if all the hounds of hell were after me. My dog had internal injuries, said the vet, and needed an operation. Bosky was put on morphine, rigged up, and the vet began to shave her side. As the thick silky pelt was being shaved away in big clumps, I gasped. There was a long dark birthmark on her side, which resembled a scar from a knife wound. I had never noticed it because it was hidden by her fur.

I buried her body in the front lawn, just beneath my bedroom window. I would often wonder if Bosky was Fang come back to save me from a lonely death on a moonlit sidewalk, my eyes closing to the angry sound of a fleeing car and a shard of birdsong to accompany me home.

I believe in ghosts. I believe in the afterlife. I believe what disappears never really leaves us. Perhaps there is a great hall of departures where the reflections of souls pause before the dark mirror we must all look into one day. In its shadowy depths we search for the best in us, to conquer our fear of entering the great unknown, unarmed and alone. As the Psalm says: 'Yea, though I walk through the valley of the shadow of death, I will fear no evil; For You are with me; Your rod and Your staff, they comfort me.'

After bidding Bosky goodbye, it came to me that what sustains us and shows us the way in the darkest of nights is the realisation that we are loved, and we love. That love, passed down by changeling wolves through millennia, exemplifies the code of loyalty of dogs to their masters. You cannot say goodbye to love.

The Mystery of Loss

On a dark and stormy night, yes indeed, on a dark and stormy night, a man with a secret disappeared from his house in Tanjore, in the early part of the twentieth century. He left behind the feudal mansion where he grew up and where he had brought his beautiful dark-skinned bride, where his baby girl was born and his parents passed, and his brother committed suicide. This is the story of Ramaswamy, my grandfather's Svengali, protector, advisor and general factotum.

At that time, Malabar was in the thick of a rebellion by the Moplahs.

One night, a patrol led by my grandfather was passing a small bridge. His keen ears picked up muffled voices coming from below. The bridge was immediately surrounded by his men and Fang was sent in to flush out the fugitives. Terrified by the ferocious dog, out emerged a woman and her small daughter, followed by a short, dark man. The woman was Muslim, and her baby must have been about a year old. Grandfather took the mother and child under protective custody. The man stood glaring at his captors who'd had the impunity to flush him out from his refuge.

'Can't we shoot him, at least?' pleaded a havildar named Pillai, who thought it was pointless fighting rebels if you could not shoot them.

'My men want to kill you. Tell me where your hideout is and I'll see you get a fair trial,' Grandfather told the man.

The stranger laughed. 'My hideout was this bridge under which I was sleeping rather comfortably until you set the dog on me,' he replied in Tamil.

'A Moplah speaking Tamil? Maybe he is a rebel disguised as a Tamil. Can I shoot him now?' the havildar begged Grandfather.

Grandfather shut him up with a stern look and called for Thiruvelu, a Tamil from Palani who had enlisted to escape his sharp-tongued mother. After a series of rapid questions and answers, it was established that their captive was Ramaswamy from Tanjore, who had left home for private reasons. That's all he had to say. Grandfather felt a sudden liking for this dark, short man who wasn't afraid of men with guns who were only too happy to shoot him.

In the MSP camp, Ramaswamy settled into a routine, rising at dawn, doing laundry and cleaning the mess hall. On the first day itself, Fang, who didn't take to strangers, jumped on Ramaswamy, wagging his tail furiously and barking and licking his face.

One day, Grandfather ordered Ramaswamy to clean his tent. When he returned from patrol, the place was as spotless as Savitri's character. You could have cut a rebel's throat with the creases in Grandfather's uniform and combed your hair in the reflection from his polished boots. Thus, Ramaswamy became his Man Friday, to the envy of his regular batman.

One sunny day, the batman approached Grandfather and cleared his throat rather loudly. 'What do we do with the woman and her daughter?' he asked.

Grandfather had completely forgotten about them. 'Did you interrogate her?'

'She gave me the name of the landlord for whom her husband was working. He was killed in a shooting and she had to flee. Her story checks out.'

'Let her go then.'

The batman cleared his throat again.

'What?' Grandfather asked impatiently.

'She is with child. She wasn't when she came here. Havildar Pillai has seen Ramaswamy go in and out of her cell. He is willing to say that in court.'

My grandfather knew the havildar hated his valet. Ramaswamy was questioned, but he said nothing. That night, neither Fang nor my grandfather slept well. In the morning, an idea dawned on him like a Vishu cracker going off. He sent Havildar Pillai on patrol, all the way to Nilambur, which was about a hundred kilometres away. Then he took Fang into the barrack Pillai shared with his comrades. The dog sniffed around and shot out of the barrack, straight to the cell where the woman and her child had been confined. Pillai was court-martialled and cashiered.

Grandfather mounted a search for Ramaswamy, but he couldn't be found. Fang spent most of the day in a corner of the tent, gazing out mournfully, waiting for his friend to return. And return he did, weary and footsore. He revived only after Fang ran in circles around him, barking and wagging his tail, in between pausing to place both paws on his shoulders to lick him all over.

'Where were you?' Grandfather asked.

Ramaswamy looked at his commander. Grandfather had never seen such sorrow and guilt ravage a man's face.

'I couldn't save her, sir.' He started sobbing, as if all the guilt in the world was on him.

The story came out in bits and parts. The woman was being raped regularly by the havildar and his cronies. She tried to fight them off many times, but there were too many of them. After she was thrown out of the camp, she and her daughter had nowhere to go. Ramaswamy had a little money he had put away from his allowance. When her belly got too swollen, he took her to a hospital. Its Hindu doctor wouldn't attend to a Muslim; such was the hatred the local population had for the Moplahs. So Ramaswamy found a deserted house where the child could be delivered. The baby happened to be upside down in the womb. By the time he was able to pull it out, it was dead. So was the woman. Just another ordinary tale of grief and callousness: an injustice was done, a woman died, the world went on in endless ellipses as the gods had decided aeons ago.

'Don't feel bad, Ramaswamy, you're not a doctor. You couldn't have saved her.'

Ramaswamy looked Grandfather squarely in the face. It was an expression that combined irony and sadness.

'I couldn't,' he whispered.

'And her daughter?'

'I found an orphanage willing to take her. Kind people. But I need a favour,'

'Anything.'

'I found a cart to take the mother and baby to the Muslim cemetery. I told the mullaka the whole story. He refused to bury them. He said fallen women can't be buried on holy ground.'

Grimly, Grandfather called for his jeep and a lorry full of soldiers. He drove, with Ramaswamy in the front seat, to the cemetery. The mother and the dead baby were given a seven-gun salute send-off. The mullah lurked behind, scowling.

'Isn't a seven-gun salute reserved for soldiers who die in battle?' Ramaswamy asked Grandfather on the way back.

'She was one, wasn't she?'

The Cow That Saved the Man

After Grandfather retired from the MSP with a chest full of medals, he took Ramaswamy home with him. Fang II—after Fang was killed, my grandfather got another Rajapalayam whom he named Fang II—accompanied him in a basket on Ramaswamy's lap. The new pup firmly clung to its protector and would accept its milk bottle only from him. My grandmother was distrustful of Ramaswamy, who spoke Tamil; she approved only of English or Malayalam. Grandfather knew nobody could last long in his entourage unless his wife took them under her wing, which was a heavy wing indeed. That wing blessed Ramaswamy when Vasanthi fell ill.

Vasanthi was my grandmother's favourite cow, a black and white local variety whose hind legs packed a powerful wallop. Sometimes my grandmother would wake me up before dawn when it was milking time and allow me the first sip of Vasanthi's milk, frothy and sweet. One day, she woke me up to see a calf being birthed; an exotic event not to be missed. When we reached the cowsheds, the local vet and two farmhands were standing by. Vasanthi was in obvious distress. 'The calf is lying upside down, it is a difficult pregnancy,' the vet, who knew Grandmother's temper, spluttered as if it was his fault. The farmhands shuffled their feet and looked away.

'Well, man, why are you standing there like a dimwit?' Grandmother snapped.

'The calf may die. The cow isn't letting me anywhere near her.'

'Damn the calf, just save Vasanthi,' Grandmother snapped.

'No damning the calf, madam,' came a familiar voice from the darkness of the hayloft of the cowshed. Ramaswamy climbed down, tucked in his dhoti and inspected the cow as my grandmother looked on speechlessly. He pressed its sides gently, placed his ear to her belly and gave a broad smile. 'The calf is alive,' he pronounced.

'Nonsense,' the vet protested.

Ramaswamy snapped, 'Don't say such inauspicious things. Now tie Vasanthi's tail and flip her over.'

He was a changed man, brisk and decisive. He asked the vet to bring methyl alcohol, which the vet didn't have.

'Then get some Vaseline quickly. Her birth canal is dry.' The vet didn't have that either.

Grandmother ran inside and came out with Grandfather's jar of Vaseline. Smearing some of it on both hands, Ramaswamy gently pushed his hands into the cow's rear and turned the calf over. He held its feet together and pulled. Its hips came free. I could see the small ribcage. Quickly, he pulled the whole calf out of its mother's womb. Out dropped the little one, covered in slimy mucus. Ramaswamy probed behind its front leg and beamed. 'Its heart is beating.' He inserted a piece of straw up one of its nostrils. The calf coughed a couple of times and opened its eyes. It got up on its hind legs, wobbled a bit and flopped down on the straw beside its mother.

'Give me a paper and pen,' Ramaswamy ordered the vet, who offered his prescription pad wordlessly. The cow whisperer scribbled something, tore off the sheet and gave it to Grandmother saying, 'Please send someone to buy this urgently.'

'Octer?' Grandmother asked meekly. Years later, I found the prescription among her things. I Googled. Ramasawamy was right.

'It's oxytetracycline, madam, an antibiotic for animals,' he said.

'Who are you, man?' my grandmother asked in wonder.

That was the moment Vasanthi chose to lash out with one hind leg. Ramaswamy went flying and hit his head on the nearest paddock. He lay unmoving, blood leaking into the straw underneath.

'Is he dead?' I asked my grandmother.

She picked up a pail of water and threw it over Vasanthi's saviour's head. Ramaswamy woke up groggily, blood trickling from the wound. 'Are the mother and calf okay?' was his first question. Grandmother almost cried.

The farmhands were ordered to carry Ramaswamy inside and lay him down in the guest room. The local doctor was summoned. He applied iodine to the wound, bandaged Ramaswamy's head, and prescribed some pills, chicken soup, mutton curry and fruits. Ramaswamy recovered fast, and was allowed to leave the hayloft, where he had been living, for a small room at the back of the house. My grandparents pressed him to tell them about his medical knowledge but were met with stubborn resistance.

'Just picked it up from here and there,' was the only grudging reply.

Ramaswamy continued to do his chores, overseeing the harvesting and staying at night on the watchtowers on stilts stuck into the wet fields to check for neighbouring farmers diverting the water from our canals. Sometimes he would take me with him.

The first time was a surprise. We lay on our backs on sweet-smelling hay looking at the constellations.

'Look, that's Orion, the sky hunter, and that's Ursa Minor,' Ramaswamy said in perfect English, pointing at the sky. His accent had a slight British clip—an observation that made him swear me to secrecy, on the threat of leaving the house forever.

'Where did you learn astronomy and to speak English so well?' I interrogated him.

'That was a long time ago, and I was a different man,' he replied in a flat voice which brooked no further discussion. Some of my most precious hours were spent with him in the watchtower, listening to him read *Wind in the Willows* and Tennyson in the light of a kerosene lantern suspended from a bamboo rafter.

One day, Ramaswamy went to Coimbatore to sell grain at the wholesale market. He wouldn't be back for a few days. My grandparents were on the veranda, me sitting on Grandfather's lap and listening to his war stories. Grandmother was peeling an orange. A car stopped at our gate and a young woman in her late twenties got out. She was dark and slim, wearing a sari and carrying an expensive handbag.

'Yes?' My grandmother summoned her frostiest voice; she didn't like strangers calling on her without her prior knowledge.

The visitor took out from her bag a black and white photograph of a man dressed in a suit, bowler hat set at a rakish angle on his head and a cigarette drooping from his lips. He held a little girl's hand, smiling. In the background was Big Ben. The resemblance between the little girl and the young woman was unmistakable. The man looked like Ramaswamy.

'Ramaswamy?' Grandfather's cigar dropped from his fingers.

'Dr Ramaswamy Naicker, the paediatrician,' she replied. 'Is he here?'

'I'm afraid he has left for good,' Grandmother broke in, guessing that Ramaswamy must have a good enough reason to keep his past secret.

'Any idea where? It took me a lot of time and money to trace him.' The young woman was suddenly dispirited.

Grandfather told her about how Ramaswamy came to be with him, omitting the menial details and concentrating on his time with the MSP. By the time he finished, his sidekick sounded like someone with a knighthood, or at least an OBE.

'What was he doing here then?' the visitor asked disbelievingly.

'Oh, this and that. He's a friend.'

Dr Ramaswamy's daughter declined refreshments and turned to go. Before she left, she opened her bag again to take out an envelope, which she gave Grandmother.

'Please give him this if he ever returns. Tell him Raji says sorry.'

'Who's Raji?'

'My mother.'

After she left, Grandmother asked Grandfather if she had done the right thing by saying he had left. 'Ramaswamy didn't want to be found, or else he wouldn't have come along with me to the MSP camp' was his opinion on the matter.

'Didn't you learn to open envelopes secretly in the Army?' Curiosity got the better of my grandmother.

Grandfather smiled. I watched a man and a woman in their sixties commit a postal crime using a steam kettle. The letter was indeed from a woman named Raji, Ramaswamy's wife. We learnt that his brother had killed himself; the guilt had been crippling after Ramaswamy caught him in bed with Raji. She remarried, but became a widow soon. Her letter said she had sent their daughter to medical school in Cambridge where he had graduated from. Now she had cancer, and didn't have much longer to live. Before she died, could she see him for one last time and beg his forgiveness so she could die in peace?

Grandfather sat still, the letter loosely held in his hand, gazing at the paddy fields slowly being glossed golden by the late evening sun. It was a difficult decision. Was he being selfish, not wanting to lose an invaluable assistant? Did he believe that Ramaswamy was safer with him, not tortured by the guilt of having abandoned his daughter who needed him? Or did he think his companion needed to escape his torment with a final act of forgiveness? I don't know.

Grandfather sighed deeply and got up with the envelope in his hand. I heard his steps going towards the back of the house.

'I've placed the letter on his pillow, let him decide,' he told us when he returned.

The next day, Ramaswamy disappeared. The maid said he had returned from Coimbatore and gone to his room after dinner. Someone saw him leaving with a suitcase in hand, getting on the swanky new bus the Condaraths had bought to run the circular route from Kalpathy to the Municipal Bus Stand. Maybe Ramaswamy was going home to his unfaithful wife and hopeful daughter. Or he was going where the road took him.

Now, sitting in the drawing room of my Delhi apartment overlooking the Yamuna River, I thought about forgiveness and the pain of knowledge. Fang IV—all our dogs were named Fang—came and laid his head on my lap, waiting to be petted. I looked through the glass window of my apartment at the night sky. 'There's Orion, the sky hunter,' I said, pointing at the sky. The dog gave a little bark, as if she understood.

Annie Besant Forgot English

As the 1930s neared its end, my grandparents decided it was time for their daughter to get a proper education. Since she was being home-schooled, my mother insisted on going to a proper school. With Grandfather still on active duty in the Madras Presidency where the freedom movement was getting hotter than South Indian summers, my grandmother returned with her daughter, my mother, to the village. Grandfather's superiors in the MSP persuaded the British collector of Palghat to provide a white tutor for her. My mother, however, was having none of it. 'What do I do with this wilful girl?' my grandmother laments in a letter to her husband that has survived. 'She doesn't want to even sit with the British gentleman because she dreads her skin will turn white and pink. She insists white skin is a disease that has no cure, and would rather retain the skin Guruvayurappan gave her. I'm at my wits' end.'

Grandfather, who doted on his daughter, agreed that something had to be done. He asked his commandant for a week's leave, packed his trunk and took the train to Olavakkod. Before leaving, he wrote to his wife, 'Dear Kamala, I have the solution to our daughter's problem. I'll start a school for her.'

When Grandfather reached home, bathed and sat down to dinner, Grandmother asked him where he planned to build the school.

'In the big barn,' he replied through a mouthful of chicken curry.

There were a couple of barns at the back of the house that served as granaries to store un-winnowed rice. The next morning, Grandfather ordered his bodyguards to clean out the big barn; he never travelled without protection after the Moplah riots. 'They've dug trenches under my orders, what's cleaning a barn?' Grandfather told his scandalised wife. She was exasperated with the new foreman who had replaced Ramaswamy, for he kept moaning about new space being required to store the grain. Grandfather, meanwhile, ordered the village carpenters to drop everything else and build desks, benches, a blackboard and a wooden platform for the teacher. Bricks were knocked off the walls to make space for windows. The large clay-plastered yard behind the barn where the farm women winnowed paddy husk on bamboo murams was officially declared the school playground. Grandfather fancied himself rather good with a racquet and wanted a tennis court too, but my grandmother put her foot down; did he think the illiterate villagers could play anything other than coconut football?

'What do you plan to call your school? Palghat Eaton?' she sneered. Grandfather wasn't amused. The next day, the painter was called. The carpenter was put to work. By night, a large board above the barn door declared in big letters: Oottupilakkal British School.

'British?' My grandmother raised a caustic eyebrow.

'We are subjects of His Majesty King George. My school will be British.'

My grandmother left the scene, muttering something like 'not for long', which Grandfather pretended he hadn't heard.

The big day came. Children from all across the village were commandeered to join Oottupilakkal British School. They were given new slates, chalk pencils and notebooks. It was then that an important question popped up. Who would teach them? The British tutor flatly refused and packed his bags. Nobody in the village was educated. It was my grandmother's maid who came up with the solution: Nonayan Master.

Nonayan is the Malayalam word for liar. My mother remembered Nonayan Master as a little martinet with upturned, pointed moustaches who insisted on wearing a threadbare but neatly pressed black coat and dhoti whatever be the weather. How he earned the designation 'Master' was not known even to the local astrologer. Nonayan Master claimed he had been teaching at Oxford when he had a love affair with an English princess he would rather not name, and was sent back to India. He also claimed King George would invite him for a session of Twenty-Eight, a card game popular in Kerala. His Majesty certainly wouldn't have known how to play it.

'The king has asked me to sing his favourite song so many times,' Nonayan would confide in my grandmother. 'But Annie Beasant wouldn't let me for patriotic reasons.'

'Annie Besant?'

'An old friend. She used to take me along for all her speeches,' Nonayan Master would say airily. 'She said I gave her confidence.'

Grandfather, who disliked Annie Besant, nevertheless hired Nonayan for the princely sum of two rupees a month and free lunch from the house. From the first day itself, Nonayan turned out to be strongly misopedic. 'Discipline first, studies later' was his motto. His first act of the day before class began was to hold the tip of a bamboo cane firmly against the wooden leg of a bench and run forward, rattling it over the legs of the children. If anyone dared to cry, the cane would be used a second time. The villagers accepted this punishment at first, as part of British discipline; when a few of them complained, Grandfather threatened to stop their rice allowance. Only my mother was spared Nonayan's violent ministrations.

My mother didn't like the school. She wanted to be punished like the other children so that she could belong to the great student community of Oottupilakkal British School. Besides, Grandfather had made a separate desk and chair for her to sit a few feet ahead of the other students. Nonayan Master would bow to her respectfully before caning his subjects, which annoyed my mother intensely. What annoyed her even more were the MSP guards. Grandfather had drafted two gigantic soldiers to accompany my mother to school, even though it was just behind the house. They were ordered to dress in full khaki drills, puttees and boots, and walk in military formation on each side of my mother, shouldering their rifles. They would come to a sudden halt at the school door where Nonayan would be waiting, clap their boots together and salute her. Nonayan would salute back but the guards would ignore him. Grandfather was ready to accede to any request of hers, but he would not compromise on the guards; the Moplah rebellion was fresh in his mind.

A month after the school got going, Grandmother decided to hold a School Day Fete on the playground. There were games and prizes, lemonade and biscuits, and even a balloon-shooting stall with an air gun. Grandmother insisted that the fete would start with a speech by Nonayan Master. He demurred, but had to yield to her persistence eventually. 'Tell the story about Annie Besant's speech in Madras,' she goaded him.

A small stage had been set up in the middle of the ground for the prize distribution ceremony.

'Fine. At the request of the mistress, I shall repeat the speech Annie Besant gave in Madras,' Nonayan Master declared.

He began, 'Ladies and gentlemen ...' and stopped.

My grandmother was puzzled. 'Go on,' she urged him.

'That's all she said,' Nonayan protested.

'Huh?'

'Annie Besant forgot how to speak English.'

After a moment of stunned silence, Grandmother gave a huge un-lady-like bellow of laughter. She laughed and laughed till she couldn't breathe.

Not understanding what had happened, the children started to laugh too. The farm workers joined in and the playground resonated with howls of merriment. In the middle of it all, Nonayan Master didn't move from the stage. 'If Annie forgot to speak English, what can I do?' he asked my grandmother pitifully.

Suddenly, a stone flew out of nowhere and hit Nonayan on his forehead. Another stone struck his chest. Blood flowed down from his baldpate and stained his forehead. The students were taking their revenge for the beatings at last. My grandmother roared at everyone to stop; she had a drill sergeant's voice when it was required.

The villagers watched in silence as Nonayan Master walked away to the back of the school where he kept his bicycle. They watched him take the long red road that ran through the endless paddy, a diminishing figure pedalling furiously into the sunset as if he was leaving his past far behind.

That was the end of the school. The barn became a barn again. Mother was packed off to a boarding school in a cool hillside town where the pines discarded cones for little girls to collect. Life went on. The first election in Kerala was in 1957. The communists won. On 4 April of that year, a small procession waving red flags and shouting 'Inqilab Zindabad!' wound its way along the red road and stopped in front of the house. Leading the procession was a short martinet of a man with upturned moustaches and a scar on his baldpate. 'Nonayan, you? Come in,' my grandmother exclaimed.

Nonayan Master pushed apart the gates which were guarded by a stone lion on either side. He greeted my grandmother with folded hands. 'I'm the new MLA here, mistress. Bless me,' he said in English. My grandmother was startled.

'I'm a communist now, not Nonayan Master anymore. We, the comrades of Kerala, have promised Stalin that we will kill all landowners. But when we come to cut your throats, I'll give you advance notice because your husband was good to me. But I won't spare the others.'

He took a neatly folded piece of paper from his pocket and began to recite in a sing-song voice, 'And did those feet in ancient time walk upon England's mountains green? And was the Holy Lamb of God on England's pleasant pastures seen? And did the countenance divine shine forth upon our clouded hills? And was Jerusalem builded here among those dark Satanic Mills?' These were the lyrics of 'Jerusalem', which King George had believed should be the national anthem instead of 'God Save the King'.

Nonayan offered the paper to my grandmother, who took it as if she were accepting a copy of the new Constitution of India. He turned and marched out. The chant of 'Inquilab Zindabad!' rose in the air again. Grandmother stood at the door for a while, deep in thought, until the slogans faded away in the afternoon light.

Nonayan Master had found liberation in his humiliation, which ironically became a gift that empowered him. He disappeared during the Emergency, one of the many forgotten communists who still lies undiscovered in an unknown forest grove; he would have been well past sixty then. I would like to believe he went to meet Lord Guruvayurappan singing both 'The Internationale' and 'Jerusalem'.

Nonayan's song was also his last goodbye that redeemed his humiliation. The paper on which it was written is stored carefully among my important papers; given by my grandmother to my mother, who gave it to me. Nonayan's pride was his gift to himself, the treasure of his true essence. I like to think he lived a lie but found the truth by finding himself. That would be his epitaph, if I had my way.

A Dragonfly Story

I believe that most children aren't nice. Roald Dahl and William Golding knew that when they wrote their books. Children are capable of great spite, jealousy, untruth, loudness, violence and betrayal. Worst of all, they can be mindlessly cruel. I should know. I was a kid once.

So were you.

Today, as an adult, when I think of all the sadism I was capable of as a kid, I wonder whether the old monsters still lurk inside me, hidden behind a polite smile or a random act of kindness, waiting to expose the bad guy I am. I'm terrified to face that moment of reckoning, which may come as unexpectedly as a dust storm before the rain. Golding's *Lord of the Flies*, which I had read in college, destroyed my faith in innocence. I saw myself in the book, both as killer and victim, and learnt about cruelty for cruelty's sake.

I grew up in a small town in a hot valley in southern India—a town that barely escaped being a village. There was no television. No fancy vacations. No popcorn, no burgers, no cineplexes or 3D movies. No video games. When we got bored, we cut class and played village cricket. Or stoned stray dogs for fun. We shot at little birds with slings and stones. We tied cats by their tails to the rafter of the local haunted house and left them to howl.

My interest was in dragonflies.

I was obsessed with them. I had a shadow then, Mani, who admired the fact that my grandfather had a gun and took me along on his morning shoots. Mani's father tended to our cattle, milked the cows and grazed them in the meadow by the river. Noticing me catch and examine a dragonfly once, he asked me shyly what I was doing.

'Look, their wings have rainbows that sparkle in the sunlight. They're angels in disguise,' I replied.

'No, they are the souls of our ancestors, who come to play with children when they're lonely. Before she died, my mother told me that.'

'Nonsense. Our ancestors are crows, everyone knows that. Hindus feed them on death anniversaries, don't you know?'

Mani didn't. He was of a caste considered so low that he didn't even have a religion. He wasn't permitted to have ancestors or feed crows.

'I'm happy my mother isn't a crow. Crows are so ugly. My mother is a dragonfly and has come to play with us,' he sighed.

I loved the graceful manner in which a dragonfly would descend on a stalk of wild grass at our feet and sit still like a pagan priestess listening to god's secrets. I had heard somewhere that god has a message for everyone, and it's engraved in your heart the day you're born. I conveyed this information to Mani, somewhat like a magus letting his apprentice in on an important secret.

'Do dragonflies have hearts?' he asked me.

Mani believed his mother had left a message for him in her dragonfly heart. He had so many questions for her, but even one answer would have been sufficient.

'My mother had a heart, she loved me,' he declared defiantly.

'Why don't you find out?' I tossed my answer over my shoulder as I walked away from him.

You always remember the first time you let the darkness in, which will taunt you with nightmares and shame in your adulthood. My time came a few days later, when Mani turned up at the house with a dragonfly he had caught. It was a pleasant afternoon, with the wind sailing down the Western Ghats into the valley, scalloping the river and waltzing with the singing leaves. He cut the dragonfly open with a razor blade in front of me.

'It has no heart,' he cried in terrible dismay.

All it had was a long, thin opaque filament which he pulled out through its tail. Whatever god had written on the dragonfly's heart wasn't there.

'Your mother was wrong,' I shrugged.

I saw rage flare up in Mani's sad, deep eyes. After that he stopped following me around. I would catch him staring at me sometimes, angrily, as if it was my fault he couldn't find his mother's message. The truth was that I was curious too, and was relieved Mani had done all the dirty work. My grandmother, a severe woman in a starched white cotton blouse and mundu, had warned me that anyone who hurt innocent beings will go to hell and suffer the same torture from devils.

'Will they cut off Mani's arms and legs and pull out his intestines?' I asked.

The question was more about myself, because it was I who had goaded him.

'If it is written in his soul, they will,' my grandmother replied placidly.

Since then, I've been scared to find what god has written in my heart. Even then, talking to my grandmother, instinct warned me that worse than doing evil was explaining it away.

'I was just a kid.'

'I didn't mean it.'

'It was just a joke.'

When I told my shrink about my nightmares getting more frequent, he advised, 'Journaling helps.' Instead, I wrote a book, my first, and called it *The Scream of the Dragonflies*. It was published in 1996. There is a story in it about vengeful dragonflies and redemption. I thought writing about Mani would rid me of my guilt in the matter. It's not the kind of guilt that makes me go slinking around like a character in a Dostoevsky novel. It's worse. It ambushes me with the tiniest of whispers when something hurts me, or when I feel life has been unfair. 'Did you hear me screaming when Mani was cutting me open to hear his mother's message?' my heart murmurs.

There is nobody I can ask. There is nobody I can ask. Mani died from snakebite when he was grazing our cows in the meadow years ago. My grandfather gave Mani's father a hundred rupees and a bottle of rum. The poor man fell at his feet and wept both in gratitude and sorrow. Today, the thought makes me weep.

Years later, when I was in my forties, an NGO I had never heard of sent me an email about sponsoring a child. It should have gone to the spam folder, but somehow it didn't. I wrote back, and got an ecstatic reply from them a week later. I transferred the money needed to feed, clothe and educate a child. The money was to be annually renewed until the child turned eighteen. My ward was a tribal orphan—a dark, thin boy with rough black hair and haunted eyes, wearing an ill-fitting shirt and shorts. His feet were bare. I didn't want to know him or hear from him—just pay the money till he grew up. I was illogically afraid Mani would reach out through time and ask me why I had hurt him. I had even found contemptuous happiness in that thought. I knew sponsoring the orphan was about trying to seek redemption from the evil in me, but also that it was a useless task. Redemption doesn't come without forgiveness.

Evil is not always Nazis or paedophiles, it is mostly thoughtlessness and indifference to others in pain. No fancy self-help guru will tell you that. It's never too late to make your life a DIY project. It's okay to be ashamed of yourself. Have an honest conversation with yourself, no pulling punches, no justifications. When you finish emptying yourself of darkness, you will be a bloody mess. But strangely, a happy bloody mess. If you're able to do that, you will have rewritten a masterpiece. You.

The Box of War

On a hot summer afternoon in Palakkad, when the sky was the colour of molten magnesium, an ageing man of slight build and upright carriage came to live in the vacant house next to my grandparents'. He rarely left the house, except to emerge exactly at five o'clock daily for his evening walk. The Palakkad countryside was beautiful then, with silver streams, canals and green paddy fields that seemed to segue with the violet mysticism of the Western Ghats. I was curious about our new neighbour. I set my schoolmate and sidekick Raghu to spy on him. One morning, Raghu came rushing to tell me the man was standing by the palm tree on the compound boundary. I crept up to the decrepit wall to look. Our mysterious neighbour was there as Raghu said. A spade was leant against the tree. A hole had been dug, its mouth a round mess of mud and stones. The man held a tin box to his chest. He seemed to be praying. With a sigh, he turned around, the box in his hands. He looked straight at me. 'Don't be afraid. You are Velukuttyachan's grandson. Come, help me close this pit up,' he said.

Embarrassed that he had discovered my presence, and annoyed that my grandfather never told me they knew each other, I stood up and dusted my shorts. 'What's in the box?' I asked him.

'It's a time capsule,' he replied.

The other day, Grandfather had read to me a story in the newspaper, about a time capsule that would be opened only in 6984, 5,000 years after it was buried by members of a New York dance club. The idea of strangers discovering objects that existed thousands of years ago was both thrilling and bizarre. For the first time, it underlined the concept of time and relative existence to a boy of ten or eleven. It also dawned on me that time went on while we died.

I helped my neighbour close up the hole; actually, it was he who did all the heavy lifting. All I did was hand over the spade and occasionally throw clumps of mud into the swiftly filling hole and kick some pebbles around. When we were done, he dropped the spade to the ground and asked me if I wanted to go over for a lemonade. I briefly hesitated, but the fact that he knew my grandfather reassured me. The first thing I saw when I entered was Grandfather sitting in an armchair drinking beer. He laughed seeing my open mouth. 'You've found him, eh, Chacko?'

I felt like a fool.

'Oh yes, he's been spying on me for a few days.' The man called Chacko smiled, handed the tin box to Grandfather and went inside to get lemonade.

'What is in that?' I pointed to the box, small and unremarkable, now dark with age and damp.

Grandfather's face grew grave. Chacko came with the lemonade, which was sweet and syrupy. 'He wants to know what's in the box,' Grandfather told Chacko, who had meanwhile poured himself a whisky.

'It's not a box, it's a time capsule,' I interrupted.

The two men sat me down and told me the story of the tin box which belonged to a fellow soldier. 'His name was Heera Singh. We fought in the Battle of El Alamein in the Egyptian desert together. We lost a lot of men, but won the battle. When the war was over Heera went off to Punjab. Chacko left to look after his coffee plantations in Munnar. I came home.'

I was disappointed. 'And the box?'

Heera Singh returned to his landholding in Punjab where his wife, two children and old parents lived. He wrote to his Army buddies once in a while, telling them of his village, mustard fields and peepal trees, and worried constantly about his daughter turning of marriageable age. Over time, the letters became less frequent, darker in tone. Hindus and Sikhs were leaving their homes. Heera wasn't planning to. One day the tin box arrived by post in a package addressed to my grandfather with a note urging him to hide it where it couldn't be found because Heera didn't want to lose the contents. He promised he would come and look them up and take the box away. He couldn't trust anyone else with its safekeeping. His two comrades buried it under the tree.

'We don't know what happened to Heera, he never came back,' Grandfather said sadly. 'Maybe he and his family were killed. So many died on both sides. Or maybe he changed his faith. I asked Chacko if the box was still there. He dug it up at my request. We've to put it back.'

'But I can keep it safe, can't I, Grandfather?' I asked hopefully, eyeing the box of war.

He shook his head with a wry smile. Chacko too. I thought for a while. I dug into my trouser pocket and took out a one-anna coin.

'Then will you put this in your time capsule?' I offered the coin. Chacko took a large gulp of whisky and nodded. 'On one condition. You'll have to dig the hole yourself.'

It took me a whole day, huffing and panting and getting my face, hands and clothes dirty. I ordered Raghu to help. When I opened the tin box to take a last look before it went into the ground forever, it was almost dusk. Inside was a medal, part of which shone dull like silver, and a revolver. There was an iron bracelet too, whose size indicated its wearer was a big man. There were a bunch of photos wrapped in plastic—of a turbaned Sikh in uniform, the same man in Punjabi dress with a shy looking woman; with an old couple; and the same shy woman, now plump and smiling, holding two little girls on her lap. There was also a photograph of the Sikh man, much younger, with my grandfather and Chacko, in battle uniform. There were two metal discs—one red and round and the other a hexagonal piece of leather—tied together with a long piece of cord. I recognised them as British Army dog tags, because Grandfather had one like that, which he kept in a wood and glass cabinet along with his ribbons and medals. On both the tags was inscribed: '1190. 4th Indian Infantry Division, Heera Singh, Sikh.' I guessed Heera Singh must have worn them around his neck. I put my hand in the box and placed my anna reverently inside and handed it to Raghu. It was night when we finished filling up the hole. A fox gave a high-pitched howl in the woods across the stream. I nearly jumped out of my skin.

I met Raghu nearly thirty years later when I went home for my father's ninetieth birthday. He was a middle-aged man with a job in the horticultural department; his sister was married to the local MLA. I reminded him of the time capsule and suggested we visit our lost playgrounds. Raghu was reluctant. I didn't give up. Grudgingly, he took me on his motorcycle to the place where my grandparents' house had been. The green fields had been replaced by ugly concrete houses in green, purple and yellow. The red road had vanished when it was merged with the national highway, which cut through the remaining agricultural land to connect with the town. The streams were dead. The people who bought my grandparents' place had in turn sold it to a builder who had made four or five houses on the land and named it Paradise Colony. Only Chacko's plot was untouched, it seemed. Just touching the boundary wall of Paradise Colony stood the palm tree. My sagging spirits lifted. When I suggested we dig under the tree to find the time capsule, Raghu demurred. I insisted and dragged him to the shed where the agricultural implements were kept. The spade was still there. I wondered if

Chacko was still around. We dug, taking turns—not that it was such a deep hole. At last, the spade touched metal. 'It's still there,' I whooped in joy.

Raghu reached down and took the box out, cleaned the dirt and dust with his dhoti, and handed it over without a word. It was empty.

Heera Singh had until then lived in my memory as a member of a band of brothers that included my grandfather. He was made real by the memories of his army buddies who told a child about a famous battle that stopped Rommel in the desert. Heera was now a myth, a memory of dead men. He was part of what my grandfather was to me. Now both were gone. I teared up. It was then that I noticed the dog tags on a cord around Raghu's neck. He looked away. We rode back in silence, both aware of a desecration that couldn't be forgiven or undone. I never saw Raghu again.

I flew back home a few days later. A small packet had arrived at home, which was left on the console table in the foyer of my apartment. Inside was a note and a cloth pouch, which I opened. Out fell something shiny. It was my one-anna coin. I read what Raghu had written, 'Forgive me, I needed the money and the medals fetched me a good price. I dug it up a few years after we buried it. I threw away the photos and sold the bracelet, revolver and the medals. I've been meaning to return your coin, I'm not a thief.'

I realised then that when I offered my one anna to Chacko, the blood and gore of Partition had finally touched us in the remote corner of rural Kerala. My coin became Heera Singh and his family's history. I put it away in a velvet case in my bedroom locker where I keep the medal, the one in the tin box. The medal I had quietly put in my pocket when Raghu wasn't watching.

The Jesus Tree

In the far corner of the rear courtyard of my grandparents' house in Khasak stood a mulluvenga tree. Its thorns poked out from all over its grey trunk—a sorry piece of vegetation, which the locals of Khasak called the Jesus Tree. Legend says the cynical villagers played a joke on the wife of an English missionary—who had come to Malabar to pitch the Lord's virtues to anyone who cared to listen—by giving her a mulluvenga sapling. They told her it was a kind of native rose.

It became her pet project. She nurtured it through the years and didn't complain when it turned out to be a thorny resident of her husband's evangelical domain—the only common feature it had with a rose were the thorns. Every Sunday, under the tree, now grown, the missionary delivered sermons which didn't impress the locals, while his English rose of a wife served cakes, which did impress the locals.

'Our Lord Jesus Christ wore a crown of thorns, and you have given us a tree of thorns. Isn't that a miracle?' the missionary would ask them.

Which is how the Jesus Tree got its name.

It came into possession of our family after the tragic death of the missionary and his wife. The role of an ancestor of mine named Puka Vella cannot be taken lightly in their sad story. It was my grandmother who introduced me to the legend of Puka Vella. Nobody knew Puka Vella's real name; his ominous reputation as an arsonist trumped any other sobriquet. 'Puka' means 'smoke' in Malayalam and 'vella' means white. It can be safely assumed then that he was a fair man who liked smoke—not of the tobacco kind but of charred buildings shouldering in the ground. Puka Vella roamed Khasak with his band of ruffians; even the wealthy and powerful Brahmins gave him a wide berth. If he was caught observing a house or nalukettu, the certainty of it catching fire very soon was the certainty of the sun rising in the east and setting in the west. He would be spotted at different locations studying the lay of the land and looking at the best fire-friendly angles the western wind was happy to whip up into an inferno. Once a house was burnt to cinders and the owners had fled with their belongings to start a life far away, Puka Vella would put the seized property on the market since nobody cared to challenge the might of the Irulanparas. Or he would build a new house on the sooty foundation for one of his preferred mistresses, who lived on the bounties of the orchards and rice paddies in contentment. He sired many bastards, and some of them grew up to be scribes, mercenaries and counsellors to the naduvazhi—the local king. Spies of the British collector had often tried to catch Puka Vella in the act, but the closest they got was coming upon the great arsonist standing with his arms crossed, head tilted curiously, an inscrutable smile playing on his lips, watching a house that was guaranteed to meet a fiery fate. There was no proof that Puka Vella started fires. Nothing would stick. The naduvazhi refused to act against him, partly out of fear of the pyromaniac's violent clan, but mostly driven by greed—a number of cattle formerly belonging to Puka Vella's victims could be found peacefully nourishing themselves on his grazing grounds soon after an unexpected conflagration. All was well until the fire starter coveted the naduvazhi's house itself. Puka Vella was the last man to be hanged for murder in British Malabar.

One day, while Puka Vella was out walking in the countryside, he came upon the missionary's house. He noticed the ugly tree and chuckled to himself, imagining how well it would burn. He also noticed that the house, though small, was a fine building. It had high walls, a thatched roof and heavy timber rafters. All these objects were fire-friendly. He looked around and noticed that the land attached to it was rich and would give much grain and spices, and the pasture would feed many heads of cattle. He strolled over to take a closer look; which was when the door opened and the missionary's wife stepped out. She had the cream and rose complexion typical of English women of a certain kind, with red cheeks, blue eyes ringed by long lashes and a mouth that was redder than the betel-painted lips of Puka Vella's paramours. He stopped in his tracks, spellbound. He lost his usual composure. The woman, missionary's wife or not, giggled at the arsonist's discomfiture, like any female of the species is wont to when a handsome man is rendered helpless by her charms.

'Can I help you?' she asked in broken Malayalam. The sun sparkled in her blue eyes. Puka Vella dumbly shook his head.

'Don't go, I'll get you some nannari sherbet,' she laughed, and turned to go inside. Puka Vella caught her hand. He drew her to his chest. She yielded, sighing gently, settling softly into the powerful arms of the fair, handsome man, so unlike her husband with his pale skin, thin hairy legs and the eyes of a fanatic. Puka Vella's clever fingers played with her golden hair as she lifted her face up for him to kiss. In due time, she gave birth to a child. Fair, with the mother's blue eyes and Puka Vella's thick black hair.

The missionary, who had taken a vow of chastity, was possessed by the kind of rage that made him an ideal candidate for a role in Hell. He locked himself up to seek god's guidance. When he came out, his wife calmly told him she was going to live with Puka Vella and their infant son. Puka Vella had wanted a house big enough to house his English sweetheart and child. Subsequently, he was seen observing the naduvazhi's house in his usual contemplative pose. The naduvazhi summoned Puka Vela, who said or did nothing, except study the dimensions of the palace. That night, while mother and baby slept peacefully, the windows open to the rice-scented wind, the missionary came out from seclusion carrying a flaming torch—Khasak had no electricity then. When the naduvazhi learnt what had happened, he promptly informed the district collector that it was Puka Vella who had set the missionary's house on fire; he was not going to let his palace be burnt to the ground. He had enough fake witnesses who swore to seeing Puka Vella burn down the missionary's place. But there was no need for the naduvazhi to worry. The fire had died in Puka Vella's eyes when they came for him. He was taken away and hanged in Palakkad Jail. Thenaduvazhi took over the missionary's land.

Soon afterwards, the good folks of Khasak who passed the missionary's burnt-down house at night spoke about a screaming woman on fire, clutching a burning baby and fending off a burning priest. The naduvazhi washed his hands off the cursed place. Nobody went near the site. Nobody wanted it. Until a great-great-grand uncle of mine bought the land from the naduvazhi and built a new house on the old one's ruins to entertain his friends, drink and carouse with willing women. Later, it was expanded into a large house where my grandparents lived.

My grandmother had often suggested that the Jesus Tree must be cut down since it was 'a wart to her eye', but my grandfather kept putting it off. I suspect it was sentiment because it had seen generations of his family born, live and die under its watch. The Jesus Tree was left alone in its place, brooding over the years that passed, carrying its ghastly secret. Decades passed since the three burnt bodies—of the missionary, his wife and the bastard baby curled up in its mother's protective arms—were found.

It was the day before Christmas, I remember clearly. My grandfather was cleaning his gun. I was playing 'pick the stick' with Fang II. The cool wind tickled the tree tops. Panicles of yellow mango flowers showered down. The dog dropped his stick and began to bark. A taxi had drawn up at the gate. A young white man with straw-pale hair got out. He stood still for a few moments, taking in the house and the surroundings. He waved at my grandfather, who nodded curtly; now that the British were gone, his transformation from King George's loyal employee to a patriot had been swift. The white man came in hesitantly. I noticed the priest's collar on his shirt.

'Hello, I'm Father George Douglas from Sussex in England,' he greeted us warmly, extending his hand. 'That's a Lee Enfield, isn't it? Bolt action, magazine fed, repeater,' he pointed at the rifle Grandfather was cleaning.

'You know your guns, I see. Have a seat.' Grandfather reluctantly indicated a rattan chair on the verandah.

The young man sat down, hands between his knees.

'What brings you here?' Grandfather asked him.

'My great grandparents are buried under that tree,' he pointed in the general direction of the Jesus Tree. From his shirt pocket he took out a sheet of paper, so yellowed that its edges had become brown. It was dated 1895, Khasak, Palghat, Kerala, India, and addressed to a Charles Dougal from Neville Dougal. It detailed the hardships endured by Neville and his wife Nora to bring the word of Christ to the pagans of Palghat. 'My dear brother, I've built a house where I both work and live, and will hopefully build a church here in Khasak. I preach under a tree which was given to your maman as a joke by the heathen,' it concluded.

Father George said, 'I'm Neville's great-great-grandson. He came to work here in the late 1890s. The letter mentions the location of their house. It is here.' There was a rough drawing of the property on which a spot was marked with an 'X'. Grandfather raised an interrogative eyebrow.

'They never came back to England. No records of them exist there,' Father George said.

Grandfather wrinkled his broad forehead. 'There's a local story about a missionary couple who died here and were buried under that tree a hundred years ago. Maybe it's them?'

'I was researching family history. Which is when I found Neville's letter. I discovered papers in parish archives which confirmed they had taken the ship to India. Then I found the letter. My great grandfather wanted to know what happened to his brother and wife after his letters went unanswered. He wrote to the authorities in Fort St George after a year or so, and was informed that the Dougals had perished under a fire and were buried in the compound of the house since there was no church or churchyard then. I put two and two together, hoping to find their remains buried here. The tree, since it is where the X is marked, seems to be the logical location since it was my ancestor who had planted it.'

'Assuming you're right, what is your plan?'

'Dig.'

'Dig?'

'Yes. And take the bones back home to England, to bury their remains in the churchyard of the Holy Trinity English Church where I preach. And say Mass because they died unshriven. Will you help?'

Grandfather stroked his chin thoughtfully. 'You seem quite certain.'

My grandmother came out, hearing voices. She sized up the situation. 'The poor boy looks tired; he must have some lemonade. And, of course, he must stay with us. I'll get the guest room ready,' she said, not letting her husband get a word in.

The priest wiped the sweat off his forehead with a handkerchief and gratefully poured himself the lemonade, thanking his hostess profusely. She called up the local contractor and ordered him to send some labourers the next day.

'How was your night? Here, help yourself,' my grandfather asked the visitor in the morning, over breakfast. It was obvious Father George hadn't slept well. He had dark circles under his eyes. He looked tired. 'I woke up hearing a baby crying outside; it cried all night. It wouldn't let me sleep. I heard someone calling my name from outside.' He sounded bewildered.

'The wind here makes strange noises,' Grandfather replied.

The next day, the workmen came. The police were directed not to ask questions since the Police Superintendent was a drinking companion of my grandfather's. The workmen found three skeletons inside two mouldy rotted wooden coffins: of a man, a baby and a woman. The tiny skeleton of the baby was in its mother's arms. Mysteriously, the woman's hair was a rich blonde, long and luxurious, having grown for centuries.

'A baby!' Father George was taken aback.

My grandfather, who knew the legend of Puka Vella, called for two chairs from the house, a decanter, two glasses, ice and half a bottle of whisky. He sat the priest down and told him the story. Father George drank. He thought. He left. He never got in touch later.

'What do we do with the Jesus Tree now?' Grandmother asked, taking the canvas chair the priest from England had vacated and pouring herself a glass of whisky.

'You were right, Kamalakshi. Cut it down, who wants such an ugly thing spoiling the look of the place? I've always wanted it gone,' my grandfather said. A sudden wind rustled in the leaves, expressing disapproval; it was not a windy day.

'It's the child, isn't it? We never knew it was there,' my grandmother said kindly. My grandfather grunted.

'Leave it alone. So what if it's cursed? It's our own cursed tree,' she consoled her husband.

In 1952, the great physicist Erwin Schrödinger gave a lecture in Dublin. He theorised that different histories are not alternative stories but actually happened simultaneously. His experiment involved sealing a cat in a box with an instrument which had a 50–50 chance of killing it. Until the box is opened and the cat can be seen, it is considered to be simultaneously alive and dead— its two states exist in separate domains of reality. Observation is the critical point: the animal's double quantum states will collapse into either an alive or dead cat the moment the box is opened and the cat is seen by human eyes. Should the multiverse exist, the same people part in different periods and different dimensions, but in parallel worlds. In one existence, the missionary and his wife left nothing behind except a thorny tree. In the current reality, Father George left Khasak without saying farewell to his long-lost family. Had he asked Schrödinger, he would have been told that they were alive simultaneously but in different realities. Perhaps this could be consolation for Gladys Staines whose husband Graham and their two young sons, Philip and Timothy, were burnt to death by fanatics while sleeping in their van in a jungle in Odisha.

The Bible doesn't mention Schrödinger, but Father George's dogged determination to lay down his ancestral burden freed his soul from an alternate reality. When you discover legacies that others have left for you, good or bad, do them justice in this world or the next.

Lots of people don't. Or can't. Care to try?

The Breathing Hill

I was born into a generation that was lucky enough to be loved and pampered, not just by our grandmothers but also by our great grandmothers. In the 1880s, Malayali girls were married off by their parents early, sometimes as young as nine or ten. The grooms weren't much older; my great grandfather Irulanpara Chami was fifteen when he wed my great grandmother Kalyani who had just turned thirteen. She was touching sixty when I was born; after my grandmother, I loved being with her the most.

My unlettered great grandmother could describe life with the flair of a Malayali Jane Austen and the eye of Frida Kahlo. When she told me about the first time she saw her husband's home, and how she felt both intimidated and proud, I could picture her getting off her luxurious bullock carriage; a diminutive brown girl adorned with layers of gold jewellery from neck to hip, and shining black hair that reached below her waist and hid her naked back. There was a precise sequence in which gold chains, bracelets, chokers and other neck pieces were worn then. The specific order is known only to a group of female experts who are long gone, the knowledge having disappeared with them.

'You never wore a blouse even then, Valiyamme?' I was scandalised. My great grandmother giggled like a little girl. Till the day she died, she concealed her chest under a long white cloth looped from waist to neck and gathered around her shoulders. 'I preferred gold then,' she said. She had a toothless but mischievous smile, and wore massive gold ear studs that forced her earlobes to droop.

'Tell me again what happened when you got out of your carriage,' I insisted. I never tired of hearing the story.

'Chamiyar told me later that I looked like a golden goddess. He and his brothers were waiting for me at the gate,' Valiyamma grinned again.

Chamiyar was her husband, my great grandfather. I couldn't imagine the stern man I knew saying something as romantic as that, but I let it go.

The seat of my great grandfather's clan was Irulanpara Tharavadu, a massive four-wing structure with iron-studded wooden doors the height of a full-grown tusker. It stood on a small hillock, a fort that frowned down upon a chartreuse swathe of paddy and sugarcane, and thick woods teeming with deer and wild fowl. A long sickle of silver water curved its way through endless acreage, making the land fertile and generous. Below and behind the hill were thatched settlements of kudiyans, or tenant farmers, and adimas, or slaves, who could be transferred to a new owner, should the land be sold. They, however, adored the Irulanpara family—Ezhavas who knew how the high-caste Namboodiris treated their workers—because they were well looked after. No tenant farmer was beaten or denied his share, no adima treated as a slave or sold. Their women did not have to go barebreasted, which was the law imposed on the lower castes. This generosity and respect brought the Irulanparas undying loyalty from their servitors.

The majority of scholarly work on caste in Kerala misses out on the numerous exceptions and nuances of the times. For example, portraits of the seventeenth-century Ezhava physician and botanist Itty Achudan show him dressed like an upper-caste Hindu, wearing ear studs and hair tied in a knotted tuft to the left of his head; he also wore a melmundu covering his torso like upper-caste men did.

Caste or no caste, the Irulanpara code was 'might is right'—a point of view Chami heartily endorsed during the Kalpathy temple entry struggle. But all that was to come years later.

My great grandmother's first night in the hill fort was frightening. She slept on a mattress on the floor in the same room as her mother-in-law, since she hadn't entered puberty yet. It had been a long journey by bullock cart; she was bone tired. Barely had she sunk into sleep when the floor began to breathe. 'It started as a low moan, which spread through the earth below. It was the sound of Hell. I was sure underneath lay a world of shaitans where a huge wind was making the hillside tremble. I was afraid my husband's family were a group of devils who ruled hell,' she whispered theatrically. I was lying in her lap, soothed by the gentle movement of the attukattil, the swinging beds one finds in most Kerala homes.

'Hell, Valiyamme? Did you really see shaitans or only hear them?' I asked in wonder.

'The only shaitans were the men of Irulanparatharavadu,' she answered with a firmness stoked by the muscle memory of a glorious, proud age. 'The noise I heard was of cattle.'

'Cattle inside a hill?' I asked in disbelief.

The entire hill was a massive cattle shed. It had been hollowed in, and strengthened inside with beams and scaffolding to create a cavity large enough for hundreds of cattle. They were stolen from all over the region, irrespective of the caste of the owners—freeholders, farmsteads, Nair tharavadus—and herded straight into the Irulanpara Aladdin's cave. Cattle was wealth, and if you didn't have to pay for it, even better. That's how Veliyama described the Irulanpara family, and how it became a tharavadu of powerful landlords. Those were lawless days in British Malabar, where the white collectors were only interested in the taxes coming on time, and turned a blind eye to caste customs and brigandry until they became too savage to ignore.

Irulanpara Krishnan, the head of the clan then, was a colossal man, almost seven feet tall, with muscles the size of boulders. Dark-skinned and wearing a hair knot like any upper-caste jemmi, his favourite method to get what he wanted was brute force, including murder, or at least promises of murder. Overnight, pattams or land deeds for hundreds of acres were transferred to Irulanpara. Nair tharavadus and Namboodiri illams were plundered at night by masked bandits who carried off gold, vessels and silver ornaments, vanishing back into the darkness as swiftly as they appeared. The native police were bribed or intimidated. Even collectors could be influenced with the right inducements because many of them were from poor English families, and had come to India to make their fortune. Hence, most petitions from upper-caste plaintiffs never reached Fort St George, the seat of the mighty Madras Presidency, which administered the rule of law. The administration's only condition was that no temple must be looted and no upper-caste men be killed. Krishnan and his band of merry men were fine with it. Until, one day, a Brahmin priest scolded him for passing the temple during the time of worship; a blasphemous act no low-caste person could ever dare commit.

Hindu temples being out of bounds for everyone except Brahmins, Nairs and associated castes, Krishnan thought hard and long about the priest's injunction. The next morning, he took his bullock carriage down the road that passed the village temple on the pretext of going to inspect his paddy crop. On his way back, his path was blocked by the priest, the local Namboodiri jemmi and a group of men armed with stout sticks and sickles. Krishnan reined in his bulls and politely asked what the matter was. 'You dare to ask me what the matter is? You have made both this road and temple impure,' the Namboodiri hyperventilated. Krishnan made his apologies, promised not to repeat the offence and went home whistling. The next day, in the afternoon, the priest and his assistants found that the temple road was blocked by a massive bullock carriage whose yoke was stuck in the mud. The two bulls were resting in the shade of the temple tree, animals having no caste. Krishnan lounged under a banyan tree watching his men play kilithattu.

'Is this your cart, Krishnan?' the priest demanded to know.

'Yes, it is, my lord. The bulls escaped and toppled the carriage.'

'Come over here and remove it immediately.'

'I can't, my lord, you have prohibited me from walking on this road or going anywhere near the temple.'

The priest was stuck. The hour of lighting the afternoon lamps, and bathing and dressing the idol was approaching. Soon, devotees would be arriving with offerings and coins. The priest was torn between caste and greed.

'Very well, remove it, but make it fast,' he snapped.

'And the bulls? Can't remove the cart without the bulls.' He pointed at the two huge beasts lying in the shade of the banyan tree.

'Take them, too, and just get away from here,' the priest shouted, his face red with rage.

That is how Irulanpara Chami and his band of merry men broke an age-old taboo and entered a Hindu temple, which would have assured certain death for any Ezhava otherwise. In the process, my ancestor and his cohort bid goodbye to an ancient evil, which was finally laid in the ground by a heretic descendant a couple of generations later.

The Parable of Thomas and John

The Sacred Heart Cathedral stands opposite a busy traffic circle, a stone's throw away from the colonial-era New Delhi Post Office, ministering to Delhi's Catholic sinners. One morning, I drove to the cathedral on a private mission. On the eve of her death, my grandmother had given me a task: perform a memorial prayer at Mass on her father's death anniversary. Father Joseph was waiting for me. I had called beforehand.

'My gout is bad today,' the good priest complained. I suspected that the rich, red sacramental wine had something to do with it. We entered the church, treading the long carpet that ran past the pews below the high-vaulted ceiling. The morning sun came in through the stained-glass windows, lighting up the arches and the columns red, green and gold.

Father Joseph made the sign of the cross and said, 'The usual Mass to be offered the coming Sunday?'

I nodded. 'Come, Father, let's praise god together, as usual,' I said.

We knelt before the altar and intoned, 'Yea, though I walk through the valley of the shadow of death, I will fear no evil; For You are with me; Your rod and Your staff, they comfort me.'

'Om Tryambak Yajamahe Sugandhim Pushtee-Vardhanam Urvarukmeva Bandhanaan Mrtyoh-Mrukshiya Maa Mmrataat.'

We chanted both prayers, one after the other, in different languages that united two timeless faiths. When we finished, Father Joseph said, 'That was rather refreshing, although unusual.'

'We were telling Death to shove off. Isn't that the best way to celebrate life?'

Every time I stepped out of the cathedral's door and strolled in the well-tended cemetery at the back, treading the shadows of a thousand deaths and the lost valleys of dreams, the memory of meeting my great grandfather for the last time would come to me. It was morning, I remember; the school holidays had started. I was staying with my grandparents. Woken up by an unfamiliar song outside, I rushed to my grandmother's room. She was at her dressing table, bathed and perfumed, combing her long black hair in which some grey had made a guest appearance.

'Can you hear that, Grandma?' I asked. 'What is Amazing Grace?'

'What's happening right now is,' she choked on a sound that was half sob and half a laugh of relief, 'your great grandfather is here. Come, let's meet him.'

A tall, wide-shouldered man with grey hair shaved close to his skull, dressed in a white dhoti and a cotton shirt, stood in the front yard holding an open Bible. His fellow singer was a carbon copy, but shorter. Their powerful voices soared up towards the sky. 'Amazing grace, how sweet the sound ...'

My grandmother ran up to the tall man and hugged him tight. Embarrassed by the attention, he pushed her away and told the other singer, 'John, this is my daughter, Kamala.'

'Kamala, here is my friend,' he said, patting the stranger's shoulder. 'I owe him my life.'

'Oh, it's nothing, Thomas, do unto others what was done for you,' the stranger said, smiling at my grandmother.

'That's not exactly how the Bible puts it, John, but it'll do.'

'Who is Thomas?' my grandmother asked.

'Me,' replied my great grandfather.

Grandmother was struck speechless, a rare thing to behold.

It is complicated, the new Thomas explained. They were from Irulanparatharavadu; Ezhava landlords of the 1880s and early 1890s who owned vast tracts of paddy and a host of tenant farmers, labourers and slaves. Nobody stood in their way except one force: caste. In everything there is a pecking order, made either by man or beast, which maintains balance or perpetuates imbalance. Had it been the 1900s, reciting the Gayatri mantra in Kerala would have earned me a flogging, a spell in prison, my tongue cut out and hot lead poured into my ears since it was forbidden for members of lower castes to hear Sanskrit, let alone speak it. Great grandfather, who had passed out of Presidency College with honours in physics, didn't see how paunchy men with side tufts, and their estate managers with education as narrow as their minds, could stop a man who knew Newton's theory and could read Euclid's translation in Latin from hearing Sanskrit. He joined the Ezhava Temple Entry movement.

One day in 1932, he and a group of friends of all castes, including reform-minded Nairs, barged into the Ganapathy temple in a Brahmin agraharam named Kalpathy in Palakkad. A violent struggle broke out between them, and the Brahmins and their assistants; blows were traded, and sticks and stones used liberally. The agitators lost. Great grandfather was flung outside the agraharam premises and left for dead. As luck would have it, a passing vegetable-seller put him in the back of his cart, took him to the government hospital and stayed with him until he recovered.

A couple of years later, Great grandfather was sitting on the Calicut beach, smoking and contemplating the absurdities of life. He didn't belong to his old world anymore; nor could he make a new world for himself. As he watched the dipping sun darken the waters, he spied a man wading into the sea, obviously planning to drown himself. My great grandfather rushed to pull him out of the water. By a strange coincidence, the man happened to be his former saviour, the vegetable-seller. A few days earlier, the man had been attacked by robbers in the Malampuzha forest. They took his daughter away, slit his wife's throat and left him bleeding on the ground.

The two men talked for hours, about the cruelty of god and men, the ironies of destiny, and a system that makes good men suffer and bad ones thrive. They didn't realise it was dawn until they heard the milkmen on their bicycles.

'I don't believe in god anymore,' the vegetable-seller declared.

'I never did,' Great grandfather laughed.

Suddenly they heard the pealing of church bells, swings of sound that swept the morning air like a pendulum of melody.

'Let's find out if their god will accept us. He wouldn't have been allowed into a temple either,' Great grandfather joked as they walked in the direction of the bells. That is how they became Thomas and John.

I don't know what happened to John, but Thomas went mad, wandering half naked on the roads and scaring women and children away. He had slipped into a world only he could make sense of, alternating between the peaceful pastures of the shepherd of his soul and the darkness that haunted him with nightmares of dying by a temple road. He spent his last days chained to the wooden bars of the barn, screaming and shaking his manacled fists against gods that weren't his.

Everyone in this story is dead. The clan had dispersed, and different branches of the family lived in different towns and cities. I inherited the house on the hill from my grandfather, who had moved to the nearby town after he left the police force. It was a ruin waiting for a buyer. But a legacy is an inheritance as well.

One day, I was conducting job interviews for a couple of junior posts. One of them was a thin young man with a lisp; he was at the bottom of the list. 'I'm Saji. I know who you are,' he said in a tone that suggested familiarity. It annoyed me.

'I don't know you,' I replied somewhat brusquely, thinking he was carrying a recommendation letter from an acquaintance or a friend.

'I'm John's grandson.'

I was puzzled. Saji looked at me reproachfully. 'John saved your great grandfather's life. When he married my mother, he was almost sixty. Here I am. I hope you'll hire me, at least for your great grandfather's sake.'

I didn't hire him. It wasn't just that he wasn't good enough for the job; I had said goodbye to people who loved me and I had loved. In my heart, I had said farewell to a house where I had spent the halcyon days of my childhood wrapped in warmth and care, until the screams and the clatter of chains shattered the idyll.

After Grandfather died, my grandmother moved in with us. But the house is there in my dreams. I'm just a child, playing on its grounds with a velvet-eyed brown calf. The dream soothes me in my sleep.

Shhhh ...

Madras 1925. I will tell you a story about Mahatma Gandhi. It's a family story. It is not one you will find in a textbook or memoir. My grandfather, Subedar Oottupilakkal Velukutty, one among the eight native officers in charge of the Malabar Special Police, was held in high regard by his British officers for his guerrilla tactics against Moplah rebels. In a bloody six-month war waged in Malabar's deep forests, rocky gullies, wooded hillsides and dry brush, many men—soldiers and rebels alike—died. Considered by his British commandant to be an expert in jungle warfare by then, Grandfather was moved to Madras, from where he led the MSP's campaign against Alluri Sitarama Raju, who was on a slaughtering spree against British soldiers. Raju was captured, tied to a tree and summarily executed. Those were stormy days. The Freedom Movement was spreading like a forest fire set alight by Mahatma Gandhi. Grandfather held him in contempt because Gandhi had supported the Moplah rebellion. Grandfather had no sympathy for non-violence.

In 1946, Gandhi visited Madras to speak at Marina Beach. My grandmother had been following the goings-on in the country with great interest, and was curious to know how such an unprepossessing Gujarati man, dark, bald and wearing attire that wouldn't be allowed in any decent house, could inspire an entire country to rise against the powerful British government. She had heard that mammoth crowds followed wherever he went, of the felt mass hysteria and the swadeshi fervour in the air. On a pleasant March day, my grandmother, the wife of the man who commanded the fiercest British fighting force present in Madras, took off all her jewellery, hid the French watch her husband had presented her under her pillow and slipped out through the back door dressed in a plain white cotton sari and a long-sleeved blouse. She took my mother, then about ten years old, along. She hailed a tonga and asked the driver to let them off a little away from the stage. Taking my mother's hand, she bravely walked into the crowd. Her disguise went in vain. She was a beautiful woman, tall and proud, her fair skin turning pink in the hot Tamil sun, her diamond nose pin sparkling bright in defiance. It was the only ornament she hadn't left off. When they walked into the crowd, people parted as if she was some kind of female Moses. My mother told me later that Grandmother's eyes were flashing haughtily and dangerously at anyone who dared to come close to them.

They approached the police cordon around the stage, where a soldier stopped them. He glared at them angrily. Suddenly his brow puckered in confusion. My grandmother averted her gaze. Bemused, he watched her pull her sari over her head. Gandhi was sitting on the stage, leaning against thick white cotton bolsters placed on a thick white mattress. The roar of the crowd was deafening. Imagine a vast silvery curve of glittering sand, the recurring thunder of waves, the wind tossing the thick green crowns of trees across the road and, above it all, a small, hunched figure silhouetted against the sun. A few men in white caps were jostling each other on the podium; one of them was holding a mike, urging the crowd to calm down. His words were lost in the din. Gandhi craned his head and looked around at the noisy crowd. When my mother recounted the story to me many, many years later, I found it so incredible; just thinking about it gives me goosebumps—Gandhi raised a finger to his lips and whispered, "Shhhh!"

He wasn't holding a mike. He didn't get up. He didn't raise his voice. Just, Shhhh.

A great hush descended over the multitude; a gigantic prehistoric animal slowly falling, foretelling the collapse of an empire. Meanwhile, the soldier guarding the cordon came closer and stepped in front of my mother and grandmother. Grandmother's pallu fell away. The soldier hesitated, then straightened up and saluted. By then, people nearby had become aware something was up. They began to angrily press around them. Grandmother scooped up something from the sand and held it tightly in her hand. She felt the Mahatma looking in their direction. He gestured at them to leave.

The crowd parted silently, opening a path for us to pass through. Even from that distance, my mother saw Gandhi's eyes twinkling behind his round, gold-rimmed glasses; he was smiling mischievously.

On the way home, my mother noticed the blood staining my grandmother's fingers and the drape of her sari. She tried to prise her mother's fingers open to see what she had picked up that drew blood, but she didn't let her. After that day, she wore only white homespun saris and very little jewellery. She didn't abandon the nose pin though. She hadn't totally lost her vanity, you see.

When she was diagnosed with liver cancer, she decided it was time to wind up her affairs. Her body grew weaker, and there wasn't much time left. Speaking had become difficult for her, the pain was sometimes unbearable. I, now working in an advertising agency in Delhi, went to Palakkad to be with my grandmother. I told her I was taking her to Delhi to treat the cancer. She protested and said she would not go bald. She said, 'I've led a good life, married a good man and lived a full life. I am not going to spoil my looks when I have such little time left.'

She told me to go to hell with a smile. I shook my head in disappointment and sat by her bed to watch her until I fell asleep. The morphine had helped. She would stir in her sleep, try to speak sometimes and would suddenly smile as if someone had shushed her.

The day she knew was her last, my grandmother summoned all her strength and ordered her maid to bathe and dress her. She could hardly stand, but she was the descendant of warlords and men who broke into temples and changed history. I watched as the maid combed her hair; I noticed in the mirror that the grey in it was still in hiding and her eyes, darkened with suruma, shone brightly. Refusing my assistance, she hobbled on her walking stick to her dead husband's study. With some difficulty, she lowered herself on his chair. His papers were still neatly arranged on his Victorian-era writing table as he had left them in the late 1970s. He had asked my grandmother to promise that no one would disturb them. I saw letters, legal documents and a pile of bills stuck on a steel spike in neat order. There was also a photo of her and my mother with the ocean in the background—it was taken in Madras in 1926.

She pulled out the top drawer and took out a conch shell: spiky, mottled with brown patches.

'I was going to hurl this at Gandhi if someone tried to hurt your mother,' she told me.

'Gandhi got away, and so did you,' I remarked flippantly, as if to lighten the awareness that this could be her last significant act.

Now, I am the sole custodian of that momentous memory which I knew she had hoped I would pass on to my child one day. I had no plans to have children; life was too good without them. She pressed my hand as if she understood. 'I want you to have it, because it is the only way I can share that day with you,' she explained unnecessarily.

'I'll keep it on my bedside table, Amma, so that I can see it every day,' I promised.

I imagine there is a secret gallery of legacies stocked with unexpected gifts. Gifts from exalted ones who have left, who hope you will love and honour them as deeply as they loved and honoured you. Such a gift is both a farewell and a salute to the future. They make you aware that you now possess something greater than you—the continuation of a covenant. If that isn't a compliment, I don't know what is.

I guess I will know soon.

THE PRIME MINISTER'S CUTLETS

One summer in the late 1990s, I happened to be in Kerala where the chief minister was a veteran communist. My mother had written to me from Khasak that my grandmother was dying—there was no email those days and she hated the telephone—and it would be nice for us to meet each other before it was too late. I promised I would take the next flight out. Coincidentally, I had received an invitation from an old friend to attend his nephew's annaprasthanam in Trissur. The invitation had been posted to my Delhi address more as a formality than with any expectation of my attendance. He was delighted when I accepted and promised to take me for a drink after the rice ceremony, to the prime minister of Kashmir's favourite waterhole. I thought he was joking, since it seemed unlikely that nearly a century ago

Maharaja Hari Singh's highest official would have visited a hick town in the British Protectorate of Cochin, let alone downed a drink or two there. My friend, in all seriousness, assured me like Hamlet that there are more things in heaven and earth, Horatio, than are dreamt of in your philosophy.

I knew my friend's philosophy only too well. In college, he became a communist, and had prospered through the many contracts he got from his comrades in various Marxist governments. The ceremony of giving the child its first taste of rice pudding was held at the Guruvayoor temple, where Vishnu is the deity in the form of baby Krishna. The irony was not lost on me, of communism and divinity being comrades. Had he been alive, my great grandfather would have chuckled, learning of a communist's annaprasthanam at Guruvayoor, because now, communist or atheist, anyone of any caste could enter any temple and pay for any ceremony of their heart's desire, no questions asked. Thomas's madness had been redeemed at last by the future, and I like to think his quietened soul would be sitting on the steps of a random temple, smoking his Trichinopoly cigar with his old friend John, and shooting the breeze about bygone revolutions and seaside conversations.

I arrived in Palakkad, as promised, to see my grandmother. She was ninety-four by then. I sat at her bedside and held her wrinkled hand, now lighter than a feather. She became the loved woman of my childhood once again, full of vitality and beauty, her laughter belying her sternness. Her vanity remained untouched, although time was closing in on her; she still wore her diamond nose pin like a provocation on her haughty nose. Her dark eyes had lost none of their mischief and humour.

'I'm going to my friend's nephew's annaprasthanam later, want to come?' I joked, giving her his name.

She almost choked on a giggle. I caressed her creased face. She pulled my ear to her mouth. In a voice criss-crossed with cobwebs, she asked, 'Is he still a communist?'

'I don't know. Maybe,' I replied.

'I bet he is. He is rich, isn't he?' she again choked on her laughter.

'He is also as big a liar as he was in school. He's promising to take me for a drink at a club in Trissur that the prime minister of Kashmir used to frequent.'

Her tone became serious. 'He isn't bluffing. Your grandfather took me there for lunch in 1922. I remember the chicken cutlets. They were fabulous, just like the English make them.'

I was incredulous. Mother came in and told us both to shut up. 'Look at you behaving like a couple of children. If you don't stop, Mother, I'm going to send your grandson back to Delhi.'

My grandmother sighed dramatically, lay back and closed her eyes, holding my hand. Once Mother's back was turned, she opened her eyes and gave me a wink. 'Come back from Trissur and tell me what the chicken cutlets were like,' she whispered.

I borrowed my father's car and went to Guruvayoor for the rice ceremony. I was greeted by my friend and his family with the warmth reserved for a prodigal's return. I was impatient for the ceremony to be over so that we could drive to Trissur and I could expose his taradiddle. We drove, he shaking with suppressed mirth whenever I accused him of taking me on a wild goose chase through history. We entered the centre of Trissur, where Lord Vadukkunathan presides over the town and its surroundings. When the car stopped to the north of the temple, my friend triumphantly pointed at a modern blue-and-white building which bore the legend 'Banerji Memorial Club'.

Though I wondered who Banerji was, and how his name came to be associated with a club more than a thousand kilometres from Bengal, I wouldn't give up. 'Fine, this is Banerji Club. Where did the prime minister of Kashmir drink? Here?'

My friend took me to a large, dimly lit room, more of a hall, where men sat sipping drinks and popping salted peanuts into their mouths. By some strange coincidence, all bars in Kerala are dimly lit, like smugglers' dungeons. He pointed to a large black-and-white portrait on the wall. 'Behold Sir Albion Rajkumar Banerji, the first and last prime minister of Kashmir, and the original founder of this club,' my friend said victoriously, raising his glass to toast the founder. 'He was the diwan of Cochin, diwan of Mysore and then prime minister of Kashmir. This used to be the Trichur Club, which he started when he was the diwan of Cochin. It was named after him later.'

Bengalis are great travellers. You can see gangs of them with their trademark monkey caps everywhere, at Trafalgar Square feeding the pigeons and dipping their feet in the Nainital Lake, chattering like excited magpies. I didn't think Sir Albion would have worn a monkey cap or a colourful woollen muffler. Photographs show him as a clean-shaven, square-jawed man with a cowlick, wearing a carefully knotted tie around a well-starched white high collar. I remember Nirad C. Chaudhury saying that the last Englishman in the world would be a Bengali.

However, the Banerji Club was neither a British edifice nor a Calcutta mansion. It was an ugly roadside concrete pile now, catty-cornered by loose electric wires and wedged between jewellery hoardings; it had been remodelled sometime in the 1960s. Some years after Banerji left for Kashmir, my great grandfather had been left to die on a road outside a temple. And here I was, drinking Scotch with a communist friend in a club he or I wouldn't have been let inside a century ago. We ordered chicken cutlets which tasted like chalk coated with breadcrumbs.

'I wonder if anything is left of the old club,' I grimaced after a forkful.

My friend asked if I was looking for something in particular. I told him. He summoned a waiter who, going by his age, would have been Sir Albion's servitor, and asked him for some details. The half-deaf man said his son might know. I wasn't returning to Palakkad without what I had come to find. Eventually, after following the old man's convoluted cues, and many phone calls and doorbells later, we arrived at a small, tiled house standing in a bamboo-green lane.

'Appachan had called,' said the young woman who came out carrying a child on her hip. 'That's the table from the club.' She pointed to a time-beaten round table on the veranda. 'Is this what you want?'

Excited, I looked for what my grandmother had told me to. I examined every inch of the table's scarred circular surface repeatedly, but didn't find it.

'What are you looking for?' My friend was curious.

'Three words scribbled on its side: Kamala and Velukutty,' I answered.

Today when I see any old couple, I imagine them as young lovers, writing charming billets-doux, stealing kisses when nobody is watching and making up after a fight over the man forgetting the day they first met; the Age of Instagram and TikTok was yet to come and discretion had its joys and secret thrills.

I reached Palakkad, hating to disappoint my grandmother. I needn't have worried. Thank god for small mercies; she didn't have to be vexed by the taste of the chicken cutlets at Banerji Memorial Club. She didn't have to say farewell to a treasured memory, unknowingly defiled by people who do not value heirloom flavours or the lost romance of history's sideshows. She didn't have to.

The Stone Lions

Where there is rural life, there is magic, black or white. One morning, my grandmother was informed by the cook's husband that his wife would not be coming since she had to help Chellamma, the local witch, to cure her daughter of nightmares.

'What nightmares?' asked my incensed grandmother.

'Lions,' was the stoic answer.

Chellamma lived in a small thatched house near the cremation ground, and hardly ever came to the village. But her daughter, a dark, reed-thin mute, could be found most days playing with the two granite lions at the padippura of our house. She would spend her day petting their stone heads, crooning and speaking gibberish to them as if she were having a real conversation.

'What's all this about Chellama's daughter having nightmares? Why didn't she take the child to that young psychologist at the government hospital, and not to Chellamma?' Grandmother scolded the cook's husband, cross that she would have to delegate kitchen business to the cook's clumsy understudy.

'They're not nightmares. They are odiyans coming in her dreams to kill her. These fancy doctors know nothing,' he said defiantly.

My grandmother looked at him witheringly, a look that normally would have sent him scurrying for cover. Not this time. The man stood his ground. 'I heard one of your lions attacked Kutty Nair's pregnant cow,' he added.

'We have lions?' asked my grandfather, who had just come out to the veranda with me in tow.

'I mean the two lions outside the padippura,' the cook's husband clarified. 'Anything is possible with black magic. An odiyan disembowelled Chami at night near the river where he had gone fishing.'

Odiyans are shape-shifting sorcerers, who transform into bulls and gore the foetuses out of pregnant women; they can become any animal they like, including lions, the man argued.

'Is that why Chami's family fled the village and his house is now in Kutty Nair's custody?' Grandfather asked sarcastically. 'Is Kutty also an odiyan?'

Just then the missing cook burst in, shouting, 'Help! Lions!'

The drama was escalating at high speed, much to my delight. My grandmother soothed the cook who wouldn't shut up: Chellamma was exorcising the evil spirit that had possessed her daughter by brushing her down with a grass broom and muttering spells. Suddenly, a lion burst in. She grabbed her daughter and fled. Meanwhile, a large crowd had collected outside our house with sticks, rods, axes and spades. Leading them was Kutty Nair, a balding man with small greedy eyes and a Hitler moustache. 'A lion on the loose concerns the whole village,' he said, eyeing the stone lions. The house was where my grandparents lived after my parents moved to the house in the town.

'Those are stone lions, be reasonable, and they haven't been moved since my great grandfather built this house,' retorted Grandfather. 'Why don't you all go back? Let me investigate things properly,' he assured.

The villagers took Velukuttychayan's word as the word of god. They dispersed, leaving a deflated Kutty Nair behind. Grandfather took out his Willys Jeep parked in the barn and ordered the panchayat president to get in. When they reached Chellamma's house, she was sitting on the floor holding her mute daughter close.

'She is frightened,' Grandfather cautioned the panchayat president.

'I'm not frightened. I am Narasimha, the lion,' the girl hissed.

'Did you tell my cook that you were a lion?'

'I am a lion. The avatar of Vishnu.'

The timing was just right, or wrong, depending on how you looked at it. Kutty Nair had recovered his chutzpah and arrived at the scene with armed villagers. The now vocal mute shook free of her mother's hold and fell on him.

She was so strong that it took many men to pull her away. Startled by hearing her speak, Kutty Nair spat, 'You can speak, you little bitch?'

'I could, until I saw you murder Chami with a dagger. Besides, even if I could talk, who will believe a low-caste witch's daughter?'

Kutty Nair had gone pale. He protested that a mute girl can say anything—a contradiction nobody missed.

'I saw you dig a hole under the stone lions of the big house to hide the dagger. You'll find it there,' were the girl's next words. Kutty Nair fainted.

A large dagger with dry bloodstains was found where the girl had said it would be. The police took Kutty Nair away. Grandfather drove back home with the girl, over the panchayat president's stringent objections who believed she should be admitted to a lunatic asylum since mutes can't talk and that she was possessed. My grandfather ignored him.

'Why did you attack Kutty?' Grandfather asked her on the way.

'I caught him with my mother. He mocked me. You're a mute idiot, what will you tell people? And my mother laughed at me.'

'That was not reason enough to try to kill a man,' Grandfather chided her.

'He tried to rape me,' she answered blankly.

I've not heard of Chellama or her daughter or seen them since. Grandfather sent the girl to a psychiatric clinic in Delhi run by a friend of his. I recalled Sherlock Holmes telling Watson in *The Adventure of the Copper Beeches*, 'It is my belief, Watson, founded upon my experience, that the lowest and vilest alleys in London do not present a more dreadful record of sin than does the smiling and beautiful countryside.'

I inherited the village house after my grandparents died. But the upkeep of two houses was heavy on my pocket. I decided to sell it with a stipulation in the documents that it shouldn't be broken down. It took time, but eventually a banking executive from Bombay and his wife who wanted to settle somewhere peaceful and maybe write a book or make a podcast bought it. The wife was in advertising and wished to be a painter. All the paperwork was done online.

A week after the house was sold, I got a phone call from the new owner. He said a man named Kutty Nair wanted to buy the stone lions, and did I mind? I had already heard from the new caretaker—Ramaswamy had vanished—that Kutty was back from jail a broken man. Why would he want the lions?

'He wishes to repent to the lions.' The former banker sounded puzzled.

'No, let's stick to the clause, no selling the lions,' I rang off.

I certainly wasn't going to allow Kutty Nair to say farewell to his soiled past by making amends to my stone lions. If anyone has a right to claim them, it is Chellama's daughter. If she ever asks, they are hers to keep.

A Circus Comes to Town

My cell phone woke me up one morning when I was lying snug and warm under a goose feather quilt with a hot water bottle, listening half-awake to the sound of the wind swishing in through the cedars. I was visiting a dear friend who lived in Landour, a colonial station that dozed in the shade of deodars above the town of Mussoorie. He and I were schoolmates, part of a gang of three. The third presently lived in a sprawling house in Clement Town, Dehradun. I groaned and sat up. The name flashing on my phone's screen read 'Chathunni Nair'.

'Chathunni is one of the real estate princes of Khasak village to whom I had entrusted the task of selling the Irulanpara house. My grandfather had left behind a pile of debt, which I could pay off easily if I sold the property.

'We've found someone to buy the house at last, sir,' the realtor prince informed me over the phone.

'Do they know about the flying head?'

'The buyer isn't bothered about that.'

'Why not?'

'He is a retired circus owner. He said he had seen worse magic tricks than a flying head.'

I harrumphed.

'Don't make fun of the head, sir. It is lurking somewhere in the house, waiting to kill any member of the family who enters.'

An hour later, I informed my host that I was leaving. 'It's a flying head, I'll explain later,' I said.

'I've heard of a flying head in Charleville Hotel here, but not one in Kerala,' my friend said, puzzled.

The head in question belonged to a disreputable ancestor of mine named Patti Valiyappan. His name still evokes fear among the old folk of Khasak. Rumour was that Patti even conducted human sacrifices. He was so powerful that he could summon Lord Yama, the God of Death, and force him to follow his orders. There is a certain dark ritual that sorcerers of the nasty kind use to trap Yama: the Mahishasura Yajnam. The shaman buries alive a full-grown black buffalo—Yama's official transport—then sits on the spot and summons the god who must do his bidding, because his buffalo is at his mercy. Legend says Patti died mysteriously, writhing in agony, at the Khasak market crossroads: Yama must have pulled a fast one. The villagers believe all his evil acts, which had caused unnatural deaths, disease and other agonies, had caught up with him. Irulanpara family members buried his body in a secret place after cutting off his head: Ezhavas did not cremate their dead then. They thought Patti's vengeful ghost would stay put six feet under if he was decapitated. During the burial, the head which had been set aside gave a nasty shriek and flew away, spitting cobra venom at the men. Since then, it has been seen by villagers while returning home from the local toddy shop at night, shocking them into instant sobriety. The local CPM leader launched a head hunt and died mysteriously in the Marxist Party Reading Room where he was perusing Anaïs Nin on the sly. Some denizens of Khasak have admitted to seeing the head hiding among the toddy palm leaves, in hilltop cairns and tangles of banyan tree roots.

I packed my bags, bid goodbye to my host and took a flight via Delhi to Coimbatore, which is the closest airport to Palakkad. Chathunni met me at the Indian Coffee House on Post Office Road, which once served the best mutton cutlets with beetroot sauce sweeter than a nightingale's song. He was accompanied by a man in a red shirt and peacock blue trousers. He had a large briefcase which he placed on the chair next to him. He patted it fondly and winked. 'Shall we?' he asked.

The case was stacked with currency notes.

'There's more if you want it. I just want the house,' he said.

My suspicions were provoked. I asked, 'Why? Nobody has bought it for nearly a century.'

'I have my reasons.'

I was beginning to dislike the man. I wanted to walk away, but the money would be useful. I was by no means broke, but money is money. Also, my mother was nearing ninety, and would be pleased if Irulanparatharavadu was sold.

Chathunni placed the paperwork on the table. I signed in the right places; my grandfather had given me the power of attorney before he passed. I handed the keys to the new owner. 'It's all yours,' I said.

He pumped my hand fervently and exclaimed, 'How pleased my father would be, were he alive.'

'Why is that?'

'Your mother and I studied in the same class.'

'Really?'

'In Oottupilakkal British School where my father was the teacher.'

The penny dropped. I recalled Mother's stories about the barn and an eccentric teacher who claimed to be Annie Besant's friend.

'I ran away from home after your grandfather shut the school. I watched my father being stoned ...'

I cleared my throat apologetically. The tharavadu's new owner raised his hand and continued, 'No need to apologise. When I left here, I travelled from city to city, begging, stealing, sleeping on pavements, getting sodomised by cops. Even went to jail a couple of times.'

I didn't know what to say. I wanted to go home.

He continued, 'Then, as luck would have it, Leo Circus came to a town in Tamil Nadu where I was working as a cleaning boy for a trucker. I went to see the circus. There I met the owner's daughter, Mallika, the love of my life. I first saw her when I went around the back of the tent where she was feeding a chimpanzee. We fell in love. Or rather, she fell in love first.'

He rambled on about working in the circus, learning to be an acrobat until he got too fat and eventually becoming the best clown there. Life chugged along but then came a time when circuses couldn't show animals because Maneka Gandhi threw a spanner in the works, and people stopped coming. Then Mallika died falling from a trapeze. Her father had a heart attack. He inherited the circus, ready to start all over again.

'Haven't you heard of the curse of the flying head?' I asked.

'Of course, but circus people know a trick or two about flying.'

'Do you plan to live there?'

'Yes and no. But I plan to start a new circus there. The Flying Head of Khasak will be the star attraction.'

It was. People still come from places as far as Coimbatore and Mangalore to watch the show put up by Nonayan Master's son. A circus in a haunted mansion with an underground cave and ghost cows was an irresistible draw. When I told my mother about the circus and asked if she wanted to go, she shook her head and smiled. 'Let sleeping heads lie, son.'

I realised she had let go of her childhood when I sold the house. It was time. Very rarely does one get a chance to tie up everything neatly, draw the curtains, adjust that picture frame which is always a tiny weenie bit tilted, put out the lights and lock up. I did that for my mother. Patti Valiyappan's flying head would have understood.

Muthassi Express

After I sold the Irulanparatharavadu mansion, I felt I had sundered an ancient loop that had bound many generations, of which I was the last legatee. The farewell was impersonal, if you can call signing on a sheaf of documents a farewell, but what the hell, goodbyes come in all forms, sizes and shapes.

When I told my mother that, she said we should visit her favourite Shiva temple near Puthoor and give dakhsina to thank god for ensuring the sale of the house went smoothly.

'What has god got to do with it? It was a simple financial transaction,' I pointed out.

'All transactions are overseen by god, especially the simple ones,' was her retort.

I sighed and told her I'd get the keys of Grandfather's old but splendidly maintained Morris Minor. My mother laid her hand on my arm.

'Why don't we go in the Muthassi Express?' she asked gently. I called my grandmother Muthassi; Muthassi Express was her bullock cart and favourite means of transport when she was alive. The Express was a vintage lady who needed some outings now and then, with plush velvet cushions, tasselled bolsters and an arched, knit bamboo roof painted golden. Its wheel spikes were red and black, and the wooden circles were green. The bulls that drew the cart were a fine pair of large white beasts with brass bells suspended on neckpieces braided with cowrie shells and red and white ropes. Their horns were copper-tipped and festooned with small bells that tinkled when they tossed their large heads.

Their eyes were so dark and large that it seemed they wore kohl—a distinct possibility considering how proud my grandmother had been of them. The present bulls must be their offspring, I concluded, having seen the originals in my childhood; Grandmother had even taken me on outings to Palakkad town on the cart.

'Amme, can't we take the car?,' I asked my mother. I looked at the ostentatious bullock cart parked in its own wooden shed, the yoke down and the bulls poking their velvet noses in yellow straw. As if it heard me, one of the bulls looked at me. It shook its heads. Bells tinkled reproachfully.

'If you wish,' my mother said dolefully. 'I just thought of your grandmother.'

I laughed. I knew my mother's emotional blackmail tactics too well.

'Fine, let's take Muthassi Express,' I agreed. 'But who'll drive it?'

'I, of course, what a silly question.' My mother punched my arm playfully.

I sighed again. Off we set out, my mother in front, sari tucked in at her waist, reins in hand, a slender bamboo rod in the other, and clicking her tongue whenever the bulls showed any signs of independence. It must have been quite a sight—both of us on a bullock cart, Mother scolding the animals, the jingle of vintage bells and the confident creaking of rubber-shod wheels on the tarred road. Buses drew aside, their passengers gaping at an unexpected 1960s' vision through the barred windows. Cars crawled past slowly and carefully, since the drivers didn't wish to scare the bulls by honking; they nodded pleasantly at my mother, since our family was known to most people in the little town—a bit of eccentricity was expected from us. As we trotted up the long road that penciled through a fluttering expanse of green paddy, watched by tall, dark-skinned palmyra palms that stood along the walkways like stoic gandharvas, I was travelling through a great dream knit by memory and fable.

She drove aside a bicyclist who had the temerity to not to give us way. He plunged headlong into a paddy field, his curses following us as we went on the way.

'Nothing has changed, I see. Wasn't your family a gang of bandits?' I asked Mother.

'One man's thief is another man's hero,' she laughed.

Though my grandmother had passed on a few years ago, my mother had kept her bullock cart in mint condition. The reason has much to do with my great grandmother's transport preferences. One day she was walking home dressed in starched white cotton, her maid holding an olakkuda—a woven bamboo umbrella—to protect her from the sun. She heard a car's horn right behind her. Terrified by a loud sound she had never heard before, she leapt into a paddy field in fright, and got mud all over her. It was only my grandfather driving his newly bought car who had honked to alert his mother-in-law. My great grandmother had never seen a car—Grandfather's Morris Minor was the first automobile in the neighbourhood—and thought the screaming black contraption was a demon. My grandfather got out of the car and pulled her out, mucky and dripping with dirty paddy water, and invited her to ride with him; her look of fury shut up her soldier son-in-law who promptly let in the clutch and drove on.

Trotting along the narrow, tarred road to Malampuzha, we passed my mother's favourite Shiva temple. She asked me to pull over and let the reins loose.

An ancient banyan tree stood guard like a lonely kapalika outside the temple. Blackened by uncleaned soot, the stone lamp in its front courtyard was unlit. The Lord, a dark, contemplative granite figure, looked lost in the darkening dusk.

'My daridra Shiva,' my mother said affectionately.

Daridra means poverty-struck; it was a fitting description of the temple.

'Thank you, son, for bringing me here. Nobody is around to drive me around these days. I'm meeting my austere Shiva again, perhaps for the last time.'

I ignored her maudlin mood and asked, 'Why is daridra Shiva your favourite?'

'Because he's kinder. He has no riches to give except his blessings.'

'Isn't that enough? Isn't that the whole idea of worship?'

'Sometimes.' My mother looked thoughtful.

The gap-toothed temple wall on which the mortar had peeled off had been penetrated by rogue roots of wild plants and grass. Along the temple's rhomboid sides, a few desultory lamps flickered in the wind that couriered the coolness of the Malampuzha river and the dark shiver of the forests afar. The door of the sanctum sanctorum was shut. I left my mother standing in front of the temple door and walked across the courtyard to the back. I spotted a gaping hole in the wall with a splintered and black wooden frame; it was a doorway to the temple pond. I gingerly stepped down the stone steps that led down to the water, which was carpeted with green plants. Wild lotuses with pink, fat petals floated in their midst. I heard the sound of bells.

I returned to my mother. The temple blazed with lights. The stone lamp was a burning torch; it shone with oil. The nada was open. My mother was looking at where she had parked the cart. She suddenly gripped my arm. 'Look, kutta, what the bulls are doing.'

I did. I was taken aback. Before we could speak, a voice hailed us. We saw the stooped figure of the temple priest approaching us, carrying a small brass thali with a small lamp. He asked us to come into the nada and pray; it was time for the evening aarti. In the gentle light of the nilavilakku, the traditional holy lamp of Kerala, in the flames' shivering caress, my mother's austere god gleamed with glory. I knelt and placed my forehead on the stone-paved floor, felt the earth bless me and felt a lump in my throat. I sensed the priest's approach again, and rose to offer my forehead for the holy sandal mark. My mother poked me in the ribs; I dutifully took out my wallet and put a thousand rupees in the hundi.

'Thank you for the donation. These days, hardly anyone comes here, of late not even you,' the old priest gently chided her. My mother smiled ruefully. She may drive a bullock cart like Ben Hur in the Colosseum, but I knew her arthritis had become worse since I last saw her.

'What about the agraharams close by, where so many Brahmin families live? Why don't they contribute?' she asked.

'They are broke. Most of their children have jobs in Madras, Bombay or Delhi,' the priest replied sadly. 'Come in and pray.'

As we stepped over the threshold and I folded my hands, I heard my mother mutter, 'Shiva, Shiva.' What came to my mind were the bulls of the Muthassi Express, reminding me of the story of my ancestor Krishnan and his bulls. I giggled. My mother turned to me, annoyed. I schooled my face and looked at the dark visage of the Lord. It could have been my fancy, but on his lips was an amused smile.

The daridra Shiva is kinder, my mother had said. It is chance statements like these that define our perceptions, not encyclopaedias. From then on, I would always see Shiva as the supreme ascetic, his matted tresses and body smeared with ash embodying an ancient, eternal greatness. Over the years, I have visited many temples, old and new, more out of curiosity about how religion had changed, than devotion. I have climbed a mountain to reach a goddess's wooden home that had survived centuries of wind, snow and rain. I have watched miraculous fires burn on the surface of a temple pool in the northern mountains. I've passed modern temples decorated with white tiles. God lives everywhere, all the holy books tell us. I know He doesn't care where He lives. Or how. I suppose it is because He is the only one who knows Himself completely.

The bullock cart we rode in that day, a lantern swaying from its belly, tattooing the brown road with dots of light, has never been taken out after that. I don't know what happened to the magnificent animals; they were probably sold since there was nobody to take care of them. The Morris was still in the garage. My mother couldn't bear to sell it—so Valsan the motor mechanic, to whose capable hands the car's well-being was entrusted, came once a month to check the oil and tyres. My mother called for a taxi or took the bus when she needed to get to town to visit her friends and sisters. An irony, since the bulls and the cart were doing a fine job of it before.

The reason my mother pointed out to me the bulls outside the temple that evening comes to me whenever I see the ubiquitous cattle wandering on India's roads, or blocking traffic while philosophically chewing cud.

What astounded my mother and I that evening was the sight of our great white bulls kneeling on their front legs, their heads bowed on god's earth as if in supplication to the heavens. Perhaps some sights acquire greater significance than they should. Perhaps not.

I imagine Time as an ellipse, at whose elbows Shiva waits to play hopscotch with the fates of men. Everything goes on, but in different forms; the beginning and the end are linked by the continuum of passing death and rebirth. Know that, and there will be no sorrow over parting with something precious. It will return to you in another form in another place. It is called the grace of god—sometimes poor and meditating within an ancient stone alcove; sometimes burdened with silk, gold and diamonds. But never poor in His benevolence. With great amusement, He lets men take the credit.

GOING PLACES

The Passer-by

Anyone visiting Dresden today cannot imagine that in 1945, thousands of Allied bombers dropped more than 3,900 tonnes of bombs on the city, killing nearly half the population and razing the place to the ground. A year after the pandemic ended—I was working at an advertising agency in Delhi then—I got an email from someone I had made friends with at a conference in New York. He was an executive in an ad agency on Madison Avenue and was inviting me for a drive through Saxony. He was German, now living in New York, but had not lost his love for his country. The pandemic was a dark time in our lives, when we bid abrupt and unexpected farewells to many of our friends and family. Now it was time to do something happy. My friend had invited a few more friends: a morose writer whose black humour disguised despair, a local musician who hummed tunelessly and a woman who said little but smiled a lot.

My friend picked us up in the morning for a day's drive through the Saxony countryside. He wanted to show us around. We travelled through forested hills and the green plains, stopping at wayside restaurants for beer, roast beef and Dresdner Christ stollen, a sweet bread that reminded me of the treats from Sunrise Bazaar back home in Dehradun. There were no traces of the great war that had destroyed the country just a few decades ago. The Elbe mountains reminded me of Mussoorie, or how it was, the once pristine hill town which is now a festering sore of ugly touristy shops, smelly restaurants and mediocre hotels. My friend's invitation was a welcome coincidence, because I had a private reason for being there, something I had been putting off for a while. It was night when we returned to our rooms. I couldn't sleep. I pulled on my overcoat since it was chilly and went for a walk. Strolling along Dresden's rain-slick streets, I felt like I was in a phantom city that thrived behind its restored reality, like a newsreel of an old black-and-white film visible only from the corner of the eyes. Scorched ghosts hiding in its shadows, spectral children at play on the cobblestone streets of the Altstadt, the Frauenkirche's door opening and a doe-eyed bride, her arm linked through her bridegroom's, skipping down the steps as the bombs began to fall. Perhaps the dead of Dresden, borne in sheets of fire, are reluctant to leave. The next day, I told my companions about my morbid experience.

'I've felt it too. I can hear them humming as I walk around at night,' the singer said.

'Maybe that's why your voice is so out of tune,' the morose writer joked.

The woman smiled wider. My friend asked everyone to calm down, in the familiar chiding tone of people who have known each other for a long time. We were dining at a fancy restaurant situated in a converted medieval house by the Elbe River. The singer, a Black American from New Orleans, sang 'Que Sera Sera' in my honour, since I spoke English. My mind wandered to my childhood days in Dehradun. The Royal Café, now closed, had a gorgeous Anglo-Indian crooner who used to sing the same song in a low, husky voice, to which gentlemen cadets from the Indian Military Academy danced with their wives or girlfriends. The nostalgia made me long for that atmosphere, as nostalgia often does. I stepped outside to smoke a cigar; the restaurant's garden looked inviting. I chose a bench, lit up and watched the city lights far, far away. A good dinner with friends, Cuban tobacco and a bench by the Elbe River on an honest night—a perfect end to a perfect day.

I blew out plumes of smoke and luxuriated in the silence. It was interrupted by someone clearing their throat close by. I looked up and saw a man standing by the bench. So deep was my reverie that I hadn't heard him approach.

'You look different,' the stranger pointed out.

'From?' I was mildly irritated.

'Others. They are very noisy.'

'There is no noise here. Or wasn't, until now.'

'I didn't mean to disturb you. I love this garden. I was a student at the College of Music here once,' he said a bit wistfully.

With his back to the light, I couldn't see him properly, except that he was tall and had black, curly hair. He didn't sound European. Middle Eastern probably.

'I should've been here a month ago. I wanted to show my sisters where I studied. The younger one was very good with the violin.'

'Was?'

'I'm from Syria. My whole family was killed last week when our village was bombed. I couldn't say goodbye to them.'

'I'm sorry to hear that,' I replied, though still annoyed at his interruption of my reverie.

'I'm sorry for having disturbed you. But I wish I could be like you when I am your age,' the young man continued, as if he hadn't heard me.

It was one helluva compliment, especially coming from a stranger, though I wasn't sure about the age part. I wasn't fifty yet. I felt terribly embarrassed, my earlier hostility now forgotten.

'I'm just an ordinary guy. Nothing special about me,' I shrugged.

'Goodbye,' he said, and touched me lightly on my shoulder. His tone held an underlying vestige of sadness.

I am deeply conscious of my flaws. The more I look within, the more cracks I find. I find cowardice, envy, insecurities, anger, dislike and hatred, prejudice—you name it, I've got it. I've also got good stuff, but the bad stuff outweighs it by tonnes. I wondered why anyone would want to be like me.

'Wait. Why did you say that?' I was curious.

'You have the calm of someone who has said all his goodbyes,' he answered softly and walked away towards the restaurant.

I sat there for a while, thinking about what he had said. My grandmother had extracted a promise from me while she lay dying. It was to locate the street in Dresden where my great granduncle had lived with his German wife. He was an engineer in the Dresden railway factory who believed that building trains for the Nazis was fighting the British who ruled India; Buchenwald and Ravensbrueck didn't concern India, as his letter explained. He was terribly in love with my great grandmother but was forbidden from marrying her because she was family: Ezhavas don't marry within the family. He was a railway engineer and migrated to Germany when its economy was booming. It was the 1940s, and he hadn't been married for very long. Hitler was losing the war. They were planning to visit India when the Allied bombings on Germany began to get worse. When my grandmother's frantic letters went unanswered, she feared the worst.

Earlier in the day, I had separated from my companions and set out to look for his house, though I knew my search was hopeless. My mother had given me a faded letter of my grand uncle's which had survived the century. It had a Johanstadt address. I had bought some flowers from the local market to place at the site. But I couldn't find the address. After the bombs had done their terrible work and Germany was rebuilt, Johanstadt had become gleaming towers, offices and apartment blocks. I left the flowers on the sidewalk beside a park where children were playing.

Had I, as the stranger suggested, said all my goodbyes? I rose from my bench and went back to the restaurant to look for him. My friends were still drinking wine and laughing. They shouted at me to join them. The Syrian wasn't at any of the tables. I described him to the maître d', who looked at me oddly. 'No one came in here. You went out a while ago and came back just now, that's it,' he answered in heavily accented German.

A ghost from Damascus? A hallucination of a cigar smoker on a troubled, unfulfilled errand? I've replayed that garden scene in my mind a hundred times since then, and still recall the stranger's words, 'When I'm your age, I want to be like you.'

What age is that, I wonder each time I get on a plane, buckle into a car, cross a busy street. Is it the age when I will meet him again? Or the age when he says a final adieu? All promises can't be kept because some are beyond your circumstances. But there is no need to feel guilty. All you can do is live your best, be proud of what you do, and make those who love you proud of you.

My ha'penny worth: be the man you always wanted to be, when you close your eyes to the light. There is no better gift you can give yourself than saying goodbye to unfinished business without guilt.

Beloved Strangers

A year after 9/11, I was browsing an American literary website on a still summer Sunday. I opened a link at random and found a stack of stories. I clicked on one. A line caught my eye: 'This car is so sexy looking I feel it between my legs.' I was no longer bored. The writer had jolted me with the image. I opened another link. 'So, right now, we will have to content ourselves with our letters, our words, and the odd phone call until I can get to you or you can get to me. It will be alright. Don't you think? That's what I tell myself, it will be alright,' I read out aloud to myself. The writer didn't want to get on a plane. I understood.

Lower Manhattan was still smoking where 2,996 people had died. Intrigued, I wrote to the editor, saying how much I liked the stories. I then forgot about it until I found an email in my inbox a week later. It read, 'I was so excited after your email. I can't imagine you, of all people, had the time to read my story. I'm so thrilled I printed it out and stuck it on my fridge.' I understood her excitement. I am either blessed or inconvenienced by a famous name without any effort on my part. I mailed back saying I wasn't the same guy. However, we stayed in touch sporadically.

A year later, my first book was launched in London and there were many parties where women in flowery skirts and glasses drank champagne, laughed and chatted with other guests. A writer whose name I can't recall was setting out on a walking tour of Antarctica; he looked remarkably fit for an author of romances. I endured many speeches, and made one too. There were interviews and radio talks more boring than a cruise on the Thames. I was leaving for Delhi the next day after spending some time with a friend who had a country estate in Surrey when my agent, the laconic Malcolm Imrie, whom I had named the Dark Lord because he had the je ne sais quoi of an imperious aristocrat who had borrowed a lot of money, sprung a surprise. I had to change my ticket and go to America, because he had lined up a book tour in a few cities and signings in New York. Both annoyed and elated, I booked myself on a Virgin Atlantic flight to New York. It was then I suddenly realised that my short-story writer lived in New York. I mailed her asking whether we could meet. 'Sure, that would be great,' she wrote back, asking me when I would be in her town and other details.

'This is the first time I've been to an airport to pick up someone,' she said, meeting me at Kennedy.

We sized each other up discreetly, like animals about to mate. She was syrupy and pink-skinned, with blonde hair cut close to the scalp.

'Did you cut your hair or do you always keep it short?' I asked.

'The Bakhtiari women in Iran cut their hair when they are in mourning. My hair was up to my waist.'

'Did someone die?'

She looked at me with pain in her eyes. The sound of an airplane landing made her flinch and clutch my arm. She had a strong grip. I understood.

'You must take me there,' I said.

She nodded. She wasn't crying. 'I've no more crying left in me, but my heart weeps each time I'm anywhere near where it happened.'

She told the cab driver to drive to Brooklyn, though my hotel was in Manhattan.

'You'll stay with me and tell me stories so that I can be distracted by new things,' she said.

She lived in a first-floor rent-controlled apartment, in a brownstone on a quiet street with a small restaurant around the corner where we would breakfast before I set out to speak at some venue or the other. I remember her waving goodbye to me from the window each time I left the house. I was given a spare key; she was often late after finishing her teaching lessons in theatre and writing at Columbia University, a couple of times a week. The Verrazano Bridge was a short stroll away from her place. We smoked cigarettes and talked about the lost love of strangers and the absurdity of evil, watching the river flow, dense and wordless as it had been through the centuries.

'I wanted to make love to you the moment I saw you,' she said as we lay in bed, the cool sunlight coming in through the open window glazing our skin.

'Do you haunt airports to do that?' I laughed.

'It was my first time and last,' she punched my upper arm. 'After you leave, no more airports for me. It was a spur-of-the-moment thing.'

'You were testing yourself, weren't you?' I asked.

She nodded. I didn't have to explain. We spent the week without being apart for a minute, her smoking cigarette after cigarette and I studying the way the light changed the shapes of her face and body. At night, we hit the bars in Tribeca, climbed the roof of her friend's attic and drank wine, gazing at the skyline of New York, and slept the afternoons away. We went near the two great dark craters which were fenced off, where evil had lit the fires of hell. We stood there, heads bowed, hands clasped in front, praying for the ghosts of strangers, helplessly bidding them farewell. Tears flowed down her face; she pushed my hand away when I tried to draw her to me. I was leaving for home the next day.

She suggested we go for dinner at the Algonquin, which had been renovated a month or two ago. Harold Ross, who founded *The New Yorker*, had played poker at the Round Table here to finance his magazine. We smoked cigarettes at the bar, many cigarettes, and looked at each other a lot. We didn't talk much at dinner, either.

'I want something of New York I can never forget. Quintessential New York,' I demanded, mildly drunk.

After paying the bill, we hailed a yellow cab whose driver was a mournful New Yorker. Everyone in New York then was mournful. She gave her address and we drove off. She was in a state of suppressed excitement as we neared Brooklyn Bridge with its neo-Gothic granite towers and pointed arches. Manhattan dazzled around us, in a way only Manhattan can. The traffic was light for a weekday and the taxi entered the bridge without having to brake much. When we reached the middle of the bridge, she squealed, 'Driver, pull over, I want to kiss this man.' My eyes met his in the mirror. He didn't look sombre then. She dragged me out of the door, leaned against the cab and pulled me to her by my shirt collar. We kissed as Manhattan sparkled like a carnival around us, except for the two giant black craters which had sucked the joy out of it a year ago. She kissed me as if she was going to die and there was no time left, as the great breadth of the Hudson moved with the slow pace of a giant, prehistoric memory. Then she abruptly pulled away and grabbed my shoulders tight with both hands. 'It's my present to you. You will always remember our kiss on Brooklyn Bridge,' she said.

It sounded like a line by Frank Sinatra. 'You'll miss her most when you roam,' cause you'll think of her and think of home, the good old Brooklyn Bridge,' she hummed to herself all the way home. It was my last night in Brooklyn; I would be flying off the next evening. All night, we didn't make love. We thought of love, life and death, smoked cigarettes, and drifted off to sleep.

When we woke up, it was Sunday and she wanted to take me to Central Park. I had time, my flight was at night. We walked holding hands like students, ate ice cream and fed the pigeons popcorn. We stood before a fountain and watched the water flower and sparkle. She opened her bag and took out a bunch of keys. 'These are my house keys. You might need them the next time you're here,' she said. I thanked her.

'I've given you the keys to the city, my conqueror,' she bowed, laughing and fluttering her fingers.

I don't have the keys to New York City with me now. I like moving homes because staying in one place makes me restless after a while. I must have lost them on one of those occasions. I didn't visit her afterwards during any of my New York visits. I didn't want the present to alter the texture of those precious memories. I wanted nothing in the past to be changed by the present.

The other day, when I was spring cleaning, I took out some old luggage to be cleaned. One was a black leather bag, a little worse for wear. I probed inside, checking the side pockets. I ran the flat of my palm over its bottom and opened the zipper of an inside pocket. There was something inside. I pulled out a small pouch of flowery Chinese silk, tied with a red piece of string. Inside was a lock of golden hair and a note. I read, 'This is for you to remember me by. I also found a strand of your hair in the bathtub and have kept it in a pouch just like this. Have a safe journey home.'

Tokens of farewell are for safe journeys, and the good wishes of old loves are guides to safe shores. An unexpected fare thee well is a treasure that will take you where you want to go, because you are guided by the angel of good wishes. I thought of picking up the phone and dialling New York. It was too late to call, and I didn't wish to mess with the valediction.

HILLS AND VALLEYS

The Girl with the Red Rose

The first time I drank beer, or any alcohol for that matter, was in my tenth year of school with a boy the teachers called 'bad company'. The 'bad company' was Bal, short for Balkishan Pandit. I was part of a group which, as fans of Alexander Dumas, called itself The Three Musketeers. The three of us had stuck together from class four, after two of us were deposited in a school in the Doon Valley by our parents—the third Musketeer was a dayschooler in Dehradun—with the nonchalance of swimming coaches throwing small children into a pool and hoping for the best. We stuck together, fought bullies together, shared exam notes and lusted after the same girls. School is an arena filled with sadistic little gladiators and perverse teachers who lie in wait around corners to give truant students ten lashes and detention.

By sharing such adversities, we became a band of brothers. Through the years we kept in touch, often getting together in my Khasak home, or the Clement Town villa in Dehradun, or in Landour where our third friend lived in a sprawling, charming colonial villa on a cedar-laden mountainside, for a weekend of drinking, laughing and reminiscing.

Bal's family had also lived in Clement Town in a large modern brick house with high walls. His father was an engineer in the PWD office and was rumoured to take bribes. Bal and I became friends in school, sharing our tiffin—Bal being a Brahmin was forbidden from eating meat, but nevertheless gorged on my mother's lamb cutlets with the fervour of an Israelite having manna. He was the best goalie in our football team until one day he vanished without notice. I missed Bal for a while, but the life of a school boy in his final year moves in a linear fashion: crime novels, movies, and taking girls for cappuccino at Napoli on a borrowed motorcycle or on a long drive through wooded Raipur, to park on the bridge over the Rispana River, hold hands and sometimes steal a hurried kiss.

It was a huge and happy surprise for me when, on the day before Easter holidays began, I saw Bal lingering outside the school gate, on the seat of his parked bike. He looked taller and tougher somehow, and had a faint shadow over his upper lip.

'Let's go for a beer, it's a damn hot afternoon,' he suggested.

'If my local guardian gets to know, he'll kill me, I'm supposed to reach his house by evening,' I protested weakly. My local guardian was one of Grandfather's army buddies who took me along for shooting in the Mohand forests; I was secretly proud when he missed easy shots my grandfather would have made with his eyes shut. He was also a martinet who believed boys do not grow up and had to be firmly kept in check by watching their every move with a peregrine falcon's eye.

Bal said, 'A beer will be worth it. It's shameful being an alcohol virgin.'

That settled it. I swung my leg over the seat of the motorbike. Bal kickstarted it, revved the throttle and lit a cigarette. I was both shocked and thrilled.

'Where are we going?' I asked.

'Mazri Grant.'

I had never been that far, and it was already evening. I was concerned about getting home to my local guardian before dark, but riding with Bal made life feel like a fable. Anything seemed possible.

We took the winding road through the valley, crossing the paddy fields and hillside patterned with wild flowers, until Bal stopped at a small wayside place optimistically named Himalayan Majesty. There was nothing Himalayan or majestic about it: it was a small, dim hall with a row of booths painted grey on either side: I could hear the occasional girlish giggle from a booth close by. Bal, who seemed a regular, ordered beer. It came in two perspiring bottles with labels that read 'Golden Eagle'.

'Where do you live now?' I asked, prolonging the fateful moment when I would be taking my first sip of the elixir.

'Near Mazri Grant village.'

'Why did you leave Clement Town and go live in a back-of-beyond place like that? You had such a lovely house.'

'Papa got arrested for taking bribes. He's in jail. We couldn't afford to keep the house,' he said in a matter-of-fact voice.

A dour waiter deposited two glass mugs on the table along with a cup of peanuts. Bal poured the beer and winked at me. We clinked glasses, me proud of my rite of passage into adulthood or alcoholism, or both. For a tyro drinker, I was undecided on the beer: it was syrupy sweet and bitter at the same time. Sitting under a bored fan pushing the air around with the same lassitude as the waiters, I felt the beer gliding down my throat with each gulp. Bal ordered another round, and after that, another. At some point, I couldn't remember a thing. I woke up at dusk in an unfamiliar room, cool and dark. My head, untutored in the ways of alcohol, was in the grip of a giant. The door opened and Bal entered. My hangover almost disappeared when I saw the girl who came in after him. She had kohl-lined eyes and hair blacker than a crow's wing. A red rose was tucked behind her ear

'How are you feeling?' Bal asked me fondly. The vision beside him giggled.

'What are you laughing like a mongoose for, Ninny?' he scolded the girl affectionately. 'Go make some carrot soup and feed the poor chap. He's had three bottles of beer. Never thought he had it in him.'

When she left in a swish of cotton and tinkle of anklets, her thick braid of black hair swinging behind her, Bal remarked wryly, 'Naina, my sister. She is the one who fills our stomachs after Baba went inside.'

I didn't understand what he meant, although I detected a trace of sadness in his voice. I was worried my parents would be looking for me, since I never stayed out late. I imagined them going to Superintendent Fulsom, a big, boney policeman with a tobacco-stained moustache who drove around in a Willis Jeep scowling at people. Showing fear was not an option, especially in front of Naina, whom I had decided to marry the moment she got back. Asking me to rest, Bal went out to score weed. Naina came back with soup and some sandwiches. As I wolfed them down, she regarded me humorously with eyes too old for her age: she must have been around eighteen then. However, the food was good, and my hangover evaporated.

Naina lingered by the door, her face a neo-classical painting and shadows playing on fair skin. 'Feeling okay, drunkard?' she teased.

'The food did the trick, thank you.' I lifted myself by the elbows.

'Do you visit the Bissu Mela? It starts tomorrow.'

'Certainly, if you're going,' I ventured boldly.

'Who knows what is certain or not?' was her reply, teasingly enigmatic.

Visiting Bissu Mela was an improbable exercise for me because it was held in a place far away from town, that week by coincidence, on Sunday. My local guardian wouldn't approve. A local harvest festival that involved village folk singing and dancing was not his idea of a good time; he preferred the Christmas festivities at St Thomas Church on Rajpur Road and was always adamant that I accompany him. Though we weren't Christians, many of his friends were Anglo-Indians—a couple of Doon School teachers and Mr Rafferty, an Englishman who had stayed back with his Anglo-Indian wife after his compatriots went home. My local guardian would regale them with his exploits from when he was a soldier and the women would roll their eyes behind his back because they had heard them scores of times.

'Maybe I will come to the Bissu Mela; let me ask Bal,' I told Naina.

'Are you coming for him or me?' she shot back.

For a fleeting second, her eyes filled with what I can best describe as a deep and sorrowful hunger. She took me in her arms and kissed me. On nights I stay up watching Netflix late, drinking a beer or two on a summer night, her lips touch mine again, velvet and honey, her tongue tasting of urgency.

She abruptly broke away and disappeared into the gloom, banging the door behind me. That was the last but one time I saw her. I was returning from a walk when a white Impala drove up and stopped at a traffic light near the Clock Tower; everyone in the town knew it belonged to the Mehendrattas, a rich Punjabi family that owned buses, buildings and a plastic factory near Doiwala. I saw a familiar face through the car window—a young woman with kohl-lined eyes and hair blacker than a crow's wing and a red rose behind her ear. Naina looked straight through me. The man next to her, jowly and running to fat, threw an arm around her and drew her close. He noticed me looking and winked. I recalled Bal's introduction, 'That's Naina, my sister. She is the one who feeds us all.' That evening I understood what he meant. He thought I knew. It was my first heartbreak.

Many years later I visited my friend in Dehradun. I drove to Manzi Grant looking for Bal's house. People looked at me strangely when I asked for the address. Eventually, a sympathetic shopkeeper showed me the way. The house was dilapidated, its yard overgrown with wild plants. The gate was locked with a rusty chain. I could see the doors and windows were boarded up.

I saw an old man on a bicycle slowly pedalling towards me. He stopped when I hailed him. A gunny bag with vegetables was tied to the bicycle's handle. 'I am looking for Bal,' I said.

'He is dead. Booze.'

'And Naina?'

He shrugged and pedalled away.

I drove back, taking the long road via Thano, hoping to have a beer at Himalayan Majesty. Of course, it had disappeared. I stood there, thinking about what to do next when I heard someone whisper in my ear, 'Who knows what is certain and what is not?' So clear was her voice that I turned to look. Nobody.

We live on certainties. Or else it's goodbye to order. It is a certainty that young women kiss young men unexpectedly. It is a certainty that people dressed in their carnival best gather in the shadow of a hill to watch men with caps and sashes tied around their waists performing with bows and arrows, and to see girls dancing in circles, one hand clutching the next girl's waist. It is a certainty that among those watching in the crowd was one girl, her black eyes impatiently skimming the crowd.

Uncertainty struck one day at a busy airport when I, hurrying to catch a flight, felt a glance swim out from the crowd to nudge me. I knew with sudden certainty that a smile, partly inscrutable and partly wistful, played for a moment on a faintly familiar face before disappearing into the crowd. A window opened and closed in a wing beat when the certainty of hope met the certainty of loss. I watched the fair middle-aged woman with a red rose tucked behind her ear slip her hand through a considerably older man's and hurry towards the gate that was marked 'London'. I looked for a bar, found one and ordered a beer. It was cold. But not as cold as the one at Himalayan Majesty.

The Brass Cartridge

One of my earliest associations with my grandfather was the smell of Rangoon gun oil, metal, polished walnut and Old Spice. On certain mornings, I would spring up from bed, awoken by a familiar, heady smell. Grandfather would be sitting on the veranda cleaning his guns as usual. Gun parts, freshly oiled, would be spread out tidily on a jute mat at his feet. Taking a rifle apart and re-assembling it, to me, was an act of god; its philosophical nuances touched me only when I had guns of my own. My great regret is that my father's walnut gun cabinet was sold, along with many other objects, after he died at Palakkad Government Hospital.

The house we lived in was large and wide with timber rafters and an ornamental gable; it had a red-tiled roof and eaves that protected the limewash of the walls. Standing on the verandah of the house, the doors open to the four winds, my eyes could travel across an expanse of paddy fields as far as the basalt green of the woods, where the thatched mud huts of the Pandarams were visible; Pappada Pandarams were a caste of people who made and sold pappadams. Tamil hymns could be heard coming from the direction of the temple at Pandara Thara at dawn and dusk—Tamil because the pappadam makers were from Tamil Nadu and worshipped Lord Murugan. There were a few enterprising Pandarams among them, like a widow who kept an oil press and often brought Grandmother fresh coconut oil. The dark-skinned Pandarams were as poor as god's excuses for men, but were by and large a happy people whose children would hang around outside the wall of our house to catch a glimpse of whatever was going on inside. This especially happened once a month—on Rifle Day, as I named it— when Grandfather took out his Lee Enfield carbine to go shooting in the Malampuzha forests. The shoot was a great occasion, especially for the Pandarams. In the 1970s he would shoot game with the same vigour with which he shot at Germans and Italians. Now, in his late sixties, he reserved his bullets for smaller victims such as spotted doves or the occasional deer. He rarely missed. One of my cherished possessions is a medal he won for being the best sharpshooter in his regiment.

Rifle Day was a big deal, especially for me. I would be holding the great man's hand while he stepped out through the tall iron gate with a curt nod at the villagers who had assembled there hours ago. The two of us, accompanied by Fang II, would veer off the main road and take one of the small mud paths that snaked through the bamboo thickets and mango groves, with the villagers following at a safe distance. Grandfather would suddenly stop and raise his hand. The gaggle behind would stop too, and wait. In a fast smooth arc, my grandfather would bring the gun up, pressing the stock to his cheek; the rifle would spit out a flat crack and a coma of smoke from the barrel. A pheasant or junglefowl would gracefully float down from the foliage. A clatter of its comrades would fly away in a flurry of wings and warning cries. The rifle would swerve. Another shot. Another pheasant down. Sometimes it would be an egret or even a deer. Whatever the game, the villagers rejoiced because everyone would eat well that night.

There was another reason I loved those shoots. I was fascinated by the empty brass casings falling out of the gun, one after the other, after each shot. Having carefully counted the shots, I would gather them; they were gleaming trophies to be stored away. On one such morning, at the end of a shoot, I was one casing short. Did I count the shots wrong? Impossible, I told myself.

I looked everywhere, told the village boys to check in the wild grass, among the roots of oaks and under cedars, but I was still one brass jacket short. Grandfather consoled me by allowing me to carry the rifle back and Grandmother sent out for pastries from KK Bakery in Sultan Petta.

Years later, in Delhi on a Sunday afternoon, I was reading M.T. Vasudevan Nair on my window seat, occasionally glancing at the patch of lawn outside, when my cell phone rang. It was from an unknown number. A woman's cultivated voice inquired whether she was talking to the right person. She had a British accent with a barely discernible Malayali undertone. I replied in the affirmative. She told me she had something for me, but wouldn't tell me what. I asked her to tell me something about herself, thinking it was a hoax. But she told me things nobody else would have known: my Rajapalayam's name, Rifle Day, the night Grandfather's car broke down near Pandara Thara and the driver fainting after seeing a white form floating towards him, which in reality was a dhoti that had been freed by the wind from a clothesline. I agreed to meet her at the Taj Man Singh coffee shop.

She was sitting at a table in the lounge, a small chic woman about my age, wearing an expensive black dress. Her hair was cut short. She wore pale lipstick, which made her lips look nude when she smiled.

'Amina,' she held out her hand.

I shook it, cool, soft and creamy, and sat down.

'Coffee? Biscuits?' She was nibbling on a chocolate cookie. I shook my head, inspecting her closely. She smiled mischievously.

'You wonder who I am. That's okay,' she smiled, rummaging in her bag. She took out a small velvet pouch and placed it on the table.

'Take a look,' she invited.

Wrapped in fine paper was a brass cartridge shell, gleaming with polish.

'Where did you get this from?' I asked, suddenly interested.

'I picked it up when you were not looking,' she laughed.

She was going back to London after visiting her mother in Khasak and had taken a chance meeting me. 'You weren't difficult to find, being a writer and ad agency guy.'

We ended up talking for hours, shifting to the bar when it got dark and then to the restaurant where we ate rubber parading as steak. Amina told me that when she was a child, she lived with her mother in Pandaara Thara, in a little thatched house with a small shop front and an oil chakki. I had passed the house often on hikes, and even paused to watch the white bullocks doing their endless circles around the stone wheel. Amina wanted to be my friend, but it was impossible then because of who we were: I, the young master from the big house, and she, the widowed shopkeeper's daughter. Childhood is a time of hope, a fairy time where there are no boundaries between different worlds, only the enchanted sunlight of innocence.

'It has been thirty-odd years,' I laughed. 'You kept this with you all this while?' My tone had become serious.

'It's a happy part of my childhood. For a girl who lived in a hut, following your grandfather and you around was a treat. You were a handsome boy then,' she appraised me inscrutably. 'I would watch you collect the shells. One day I decided to take one before you noticed and trade it for your friendship later.'

'Why didn't you?'

Her laconic glance was the answer. We were separated by the sadness of knowing and the indifference of unknowing; she had a treasure belonging to someone else, someone she wanted to know. By letting go of it, she was letting go of an impossible longing that was now irrelevant. Our exchange united us for one shining moment. It was alive. It was enough. And we had something that will never end.

The Mother in the Gallery

Last year, I was in Haridwar to perform shradh for my father, who had passed away during the pandemic in 2021. On the ghat, a distance away, stood a man with a brass urn. My priest advised me to take the customary three dips in the river, even though the current was strong enough to drag me along till the Bay of Bengal. Back on safe ground, I still couldn't take my eyes off the stranger with the urn; his body was frozen in a grief so profound that it covered him in a sheath of cold which no happy memory on earth could possibly thaw.

The priest noticed my interest and said, 'He is a strange case, sir.'

'Tell me more,' I requested.

'His daughter died in the second wave of the pandemic and he came here with her ashes. I thought then that he must be an influential person because other bodies were being buried outside the town in mass graves or cremated together. My guess was correct since a senior priest called up asking me to assist the man. I put on gloves and a mask and performed the puja. After I was done, I asked him to step into the water and empty the remains into Ma Ganga.

'"Not all of it, panditji, just a little bit," he pleaded.

'"But the soul won't get peace, sir. Besides, it's bad luck to keep a dead person's ashes inside a house," I warned him.

'"This is my daughter inside," he snapped. "Her mother died in childbirth, and she is all I have. I can't say goodbye to her just like that."

'I wanted to point out that she was already gone, but did not have the heart or the courage to tell him. I let him do the asthivisarjan the way he wanted. Last year, he came again, with the ashes in a polished brass urn. Now he's here again. I asked him how long he was going to keep at it. "Until there is nothing left," he told me.'

'Then what?' I asked curiously.

'He told me he'll say his final goodbye to his daughter when the urn becomes empty and then he'll give himself to the Ganga so that he can be with her again,' the priest answered.

I believe in rebirth. Hindu texts say that a soul's journey towards salvation is along a path of pain. It is the duty of the person who performs the farewell rites to protect it.

'My beloved one, here, I offer you rice to satiate your hunger as you walk on the path of Death. May this umbrella protect you from the searing heat. May these shoes defend you from the thorns on the way. May these garments save you from the freezing winds. Here, drink cool water from this pot of clay and quench your thirst. So secured, may you become a Pitri: ancestor, father, grandfather and great-grandfather, mother, grandmother and great-grandmother. Unite with them and be reborn again.'

A tragic story my grandmother told me about the Moplah Rebellion came to me unbidden. It was the early 1920s, and a revolt had erupted in Valluvanad. The rebels had gone on a rampage, sparing no one even remotely related to the British government. My grandfather was alerted about a group of armed Muslim peasants on their way to plunder and burn down the nalukkettu home of a Nair landlord living near Tirurangadi. He rushed there with a battalion and set upon the rebels. His ferocity saved the day; some in the mob were killed and the rest fled. Driving on towards the Englishwoman's house, he came across many burning houses and corpses of people, mostly Hindu landlords, their wives and armed servitors, There were children, too, whose throats were slit and their bodies flung aside in thickets, or thrown into the Kadalundi river and water-filled paddy fields. One such corpse was of a young boy whose features suggested a refined upbringing. His body lay half submerged in the river, half on the bank; he had been stabled in the chest. Blood oozed into the wet ground and turned the water rusty brown.

When my grandfather, followed by the lorry full of armed soldiers, reached the nalukettu gates, the women inside began to scream. After much reassurance, the gates were opened and a lady in her forties rushed down to meet them. 'Find my son, sir, and bring him home,' she begged, clinging to his jeep door. My grandfather gently disengaged himself. The distraught lady, in spite of her worry, was well bred enough to invite him in and offer refreshments. When he entered the drawing room that smelt of old wood and hibiscus flowers, his eye fell on a photograph of the mother and son in a frame which occupied a place of pride on a tall wooden table. He recognised the dead boy.

'He's all I have, my husband died a few years ago. Please bring him home,' she pleaded, pointing at the picture.

My grandfather nodded, but his heart was not in it. The woman looked at his expression, and a shiver passed through her slender body. Local legend has it that after the MSP soldiers left, she went to the gallery upstairs and stood there looking out through the window, waiting for her son to come home. She neither ate nor drank, and starved to death waiting for her boy. The Rebellion was over by then. The servants were sent away with handsome amounts of money. She gave her kudiyans legal possession of the land they lived and worked on. Time covered the unswept courtyard with leaves and grass. The garden, once so beautifully tended, was invaded by weeds and wild grass.

Mysteriously, the house itself remained untouched by Nature's depredations. I heard the story of the haunted house from my grandmother. Once when I invited two of my friends to spend our summer holidays in Khasak, Ramaswamy informed me quite seriously that every year, on a particular day, a beautiful long-haired woman wearing mundum neryathum would appear at the nalukattil's upper storey window, and vanish after sunset. My grandmother dismissed the story as village superstition. The bungalow acquired an evil reputation after a group of local boys, on a dare, went inside and never returned home.

I was in school at the time; like most boys in the 1970s, I was an admirer of Lenin and Stalin, although I studied in a fancy school where the masters were sterner than Moses. When my friends suggested we spend a night in the house, I was game. I scoffed at the notion of ghosts since the only spirit I recognised was that of the Revolution, although I wasn't eager to come across a ghost myself. Khasak has its own ghost stories about village demons hiding in the bamboo thickets and attacking anyone who passed at night. Undeterred by such native tales, we took directions from Ramaswamy, who flatly refused to accompany us, because he would be burnt in the fire of my grandmother's wrath. We located the house without much difficulty because everyone knew where the cursed house was—people looked worried when they recognised me; they were not keen to meet my grandparents if anything untoward happened.

The nalukketu's padippura stood with its iron bound doors open. We entered, tip-toeing across the large front court, and knocked on the door. To our surprise, it opened noiselessly. The mosaic-paved corridors, the checkboard flooring and the fireplace were spotlessly clean. We examined each room; the chintz curtains of the formal sitting room had a fireplace and inglenooks on both sides. A bust of Queen Victoria frowned at us from the top of an elaborately carved pillar. The house was clean and organised as if someone lived there. Obviously, there were servants here, who must have come in to dust and clean the place and gone back to the village.

'Hello, anyone here?' I asked aloud.

Nobody answered.

We entered a small parlour. One of my companions suddenly clutched my arm and pointed to a small table placed on a carpet in the middle of the room. Four chairs had been arranged in a neat circle around it. Plates piled with pastries, cupcakes and pudding invited us to gorge on them. 'Don't touch a thing,' I warned my friends, seized by alarm. I was certain someone was playing a hoax on us. As we hesitated between greed and fear, the shadows of evenlight stole in through the slatted windows. The atmosphere became chilly. We thought we heard steps on the wooden stairs. We agreed it wasn't wise to wait to find out whose. We fled. As I ran, I looked back over my shoulder and fancied I saw the outline of a woman in a mundum neriyathum standing on the shadowy gallery, watching us.

'Every year, on the day her child died, she comes to the window,' chuckled Kumarasan, a wizened cynic who ran a tea shop on the way. In the reassuring normalcy of snacking on pakodas and gulping down nannarisarvat, we laughed away our fears.

This is not necessarily a ghost story. My theory is that the woman's ghost, if there was one, and the grieving father in Haridwar were both looking for closure. But there is nothing like closure in the human condition. The passing of a loved one isn't a store going out of business. They will always remain a part of you. Closure is a fantasy. There is only continuity. Anyone who tells you otherwise is kidding themselves.

A Woman of Letters

'New Delhi
24 May

Dearest Amma,

I'm writing this because I miss you. And love you. How much of missing is part of love is a question that has been plaguing me for a while. Perhaps you would know the answer.'

This is a letter I wrote to my mother; it has been kept aside to complete later. I prefer to send emails, even in personal matters, because the process of writing a letter is cumbersome. It was something we did in the 1970s and 1980s when the red pillar box, always shiny red, was the medium that carried our words—loving, passionate, angry, pathetic, avaricious, formal—to a sibling, parents, friend, lover or a government officer. It was the receptacle of short stories I sent to *Malayala Nadu* and *Kala Kaumudi* magazines which were edited by my good friends Srinivasan and N.R.S. Babu, respectively—stories written laboriously on foolscap paper with pen and ink. My mother used an exquisitely cared for Luxmi fountain pen made by Dr Radhika Nath Saha in the early 1900s, which my grandmother had first used after her encounter with Mahatma Gandhi. It was the first 'swadeshi' pen. The ink my mother used was cobalt blue Sulekha ink: Gandhi asked a chemist friend of his named Satish Das Gupta to prepare a 'swadeshi ink' for his beloved Luxmi. Gupta made Krishnadhara ink, which was bought later by the owners of Sulekha.

My mother told me all this when I was driving her home from Delhi airport. She looked around her as the car wound its way through Delhi traffic; she hadn't been in the city for a while. 'So much has changed,' she said. 'Why don't you write me letters anymore? You used to when you were in the college hostel. Your handwriting was so beautiful.'

Although her cursive style of writing was more beautiful than any handwriting I've seen, I preferred she mailed me instead of long letters. 'That's a long time ago. Now I send emails,' I said.

'Emails are impersonal, I've seen one or two on a friend's daughter's laptop,' she argued when I expressed my view of letter writing. 'Besides I don't have a computer,' she said.

I offered to get her one. She shrank back in the car seat, horrified. 'You'll suggest a laptop next. It sounds obscene, like a dance bar.'

I wondered where my mother who lived in practical seclusion in a large house in Khasak knew about lap dances, but I let it go. I asked, 'How about getting you a smartphone for WhatsApp then?'

'You want to spy on me now? I read the government has bought some Israeli contraption to spy on everyone. Not that an old woman like me has things to hide, but I've no desire to let babus read my personal thoughts. I'll stick to writing letters, thank you. If you can't find the time to read them, son, just throw them in the trash.'

'But it is so inconvenient writing letters, Amma, it takes so much time.'

'Aha, now that I'm old, are you saying I don't have much time left?' My mother could be very mulish, though she managed to make perversely logical points in our arguments.

'I didn't mean that writing a letter is too much trouble. You have to first buy the paper. Then fill ink in a fountain pen. You must write with a fountain pen, which could leak and get messy, because ball points aren't classy. Then you've to go all the way to the post office and buy a stamp, glue it on the envelope and put the letter in a post box. Compare that to the ease of sending an email or a phone message.'

'Any worthwhile effort takes time and some labour. A letter is a thing of beauty, my son. Have you realised that? It is the architecture of life.'

My mother's letter paper was pure white like an egret's wing. She chose envelopes the colour of ivory. Being the vain person she is, the initials of her name are embossed on their back flap, as well on the latter paper. In my mother's hands letters became works of art.

'Do you know why people collect stamps?' she asked, turning the car's air-conditioner down, though it was summer: the kind of Delhi summer where you can fry eggs on the road. I reached out with one hand and pulled the shawl over her frail shoulders closer. I shook my head.

'Stamps are mementos from another time. The month or year some king was crowned, Gandhi was assassinated, when Neil Armstrong went to the moon, a poet died. They mark the travel of emotion through history.'

'You need to rest, Amma,' I suggested before she got into her full flow; then I realised she didn't get much conversation in the countryside where she lived.

'I'm not ailing, I'm just a little bit ill,' she protested, the old humour hadn't left her though her voice was weak.

'Now we are quibbling,' I laughed.

'What time is the doctor's appointment tomorrow?' she asked. There was an undertone of regret in her voice. I told her.

At home, after serving us dinner, Pandey, my Svengali, retired to his room for the night. My mother had taught him all my favourite dishes: kozhakattas, paniyaram, puttu and kadala, idiyappams, thiyyal, kalan, panni carry, fish curry with Malabar tamarind, irachiolachathu; I was gastronomically very demanding. At breakfast, Pandey served us neypathal—a rice pancake made with lots of ghee. My mother sniffed it and took a bite. I was concerned. Pandey was nervous.

'You don't like it, Amme?' I asked nervously.

'It's very good.' She dipped a piece in her egg curry. 'But I never taught him neypathal. Was it one of those Punjabi hussies you bring home? Why you don't marry a good Malayali girl I don't understand—' She went off on her favourite tangent.

'How's the food?' I tried to divert her attention.

'You haven't told me how you got the recipe?' she questioned Pandey in her clumsy Hindi.

'YouTube,' I interrupted her before he fainted. Pandey would give his life for my tiny silver-haired mother, but he was terrified of her.

'What tube? You're getting food in tubes now?' She moved her plate away.

I explained YouTube to her. She was traumatised. 'Food from a video, Krishna Krishna, what is the world coming to?' my mother was alarmed. 'Why aren't you cooking from my recipes?' she turned to Pandey.

'They were handwritten by you, Amma. One day Pandey dropped the notebook in boiling water. See, writing things down has many disadvantages. I would have stored the recipes on my computer if only you had typed them out.'

My mother was crestfallen. She didn't speak much. She lived alone in her large two-storey house in Khasak, surrounded by paddy fields which were watered by the Papanasini River that flowed skirting our land. After her morning prayers, she sat at her large table top upholstered with green baize, a tall window open to the sunlight dancing on the rice stalks and pepper vines, and the light violet peaks of the Western Ghats watching her from afar. She did her accounts, wrote to her friends, and penned down enchanting poetry and whimsical short stories she never sent for publication.

We drove to Fortis Hospital in Gurgaon the next day. My mother endured the scores of tests without protest, though she must have gone through hell. When Dr Amitabh Parti printed out his prescription, she was annoyed that it was not handwritten.

'Remember Dr C.V. Raman, who drove his black Ambassador car himself to make house calls? Nobody could figure his handwriting on prescriptions except the compounder, which is part of the mystery,' she laughed heartily and coughed blood into her lace handkerchief which annoyed her greatly; she was almost anal about cleanliness. I recollected the clinic on the road to Kalpathy, where the compounder diligently made powders and syrups with the mysterious air of an alchemist: Dr C.V. Raman never went wrong with his diagnosis. Like in my mother's case.

When the final diagnosis came, she refused chemotherapy. 'It'll spoil my looks,' she said defiantly, stroking her lush silver hair. 'I want to live the way I want to during the last days Guruvayoorappan has given me.'

Mother had wished to be cremated on top of the little hillock on our land overlooking the river. Even in death she wanted familiarity for her farewell. She became ash, taken by the wind to scatter on the gentle flow of the Papanasini—the small ghat with ash-black stone steps where she would bathe; in whose waters we cooled beer bottles, read detective stories lying on a hammock that stooped so low over the water we could touch the flow. As I watched the white smoke of the last of her spreading in the Khasak wind, I was happy she had lived and died in a place she loved. Going through her room, I came across a wooden chest. I unlocked the clasp and opened the lid. The box was filled with scores of packets, each one tied with different coloured silk ribbons. They were letters. I sat on her chair and opened the packets one by one. The sun had set by the time I finished; so engrossed was I that I forgot lunch. The letters were the history of my family. The oldest one was in the late 1800s, from my unlettered great great grandmother to her husband about the death of a milch cow—she had obviously got an ezhuthachan to write it for her; ezhuthachans were professional scribes who wrote dictated messages for a fee. There was one from my grandmother with a faded tear stain on its margin, to my great uncle explaining why she couldn't marry him; obviously, she hadn't posted it because there was no address on the Air Mail envelope. There were letters from my grandfather to my grandmother, complaining about how hot Africa was, and later how the Moplahagitationists were being wiped out; my grandmother's account to her husband of goings-on in Oottupilakkal British School; love letters from my father to my mother; from me to her groaning about food in the college hostel; an anxious letter from my uncle to my mother asking about her sickness. They were either funny, wistful, sad, joyous or drily boring like the reply from an accountant to my great grandfather about the sale of a piece of land. My mother was right. I was reading centuries of familial history. The letters were the architecture of our lives.

My mother's will left everything to me, except for a few generous bequests to old servants and a distant cousin. The most precious of her gifts to me was her Luxmi swadeshi pen. I took the letters back home to Delhi. I got creamy stationery and got my initials engraved on them. Every week, I would sit down to write a letter to my mother. I would tell her about what was happening to me: work intrigues, girlfriends, travels, dinners; I was adding to the unique architecture of an ancient family. I never posted them obviously. I added each letter to a growing pile of letters, wrapped in a blue silk ribbon; blue being my mother's favourite colour. I was writing her a farewell, one that would last until I went to sleep on the little hillock overlooking the Papanasini River.

THE MAJOR MORRIS

After Mother's tryst with the Papanasini, there was nothing left to keep me in Khasak. She had found it difficult to maintain the house and the farmland, since after the 1950s, Communist thugs bullied landowners to hire only party workers to till the fields; lamentably, the previous work ethic of union workers had disappeared after the Land Reform Act. Now new landowners, the workers hid an ancient inferiority complex under mulish ideology and became either alcoholics or MLAs—or both. The Kerala class war was helping neither them nor the landholders as the state began its slow decline into economic ruin. The smarter landlords joined the Party, became politicians and forced their former serfs and now current comrades to work even harder than before. I had no desire to be trapped by ideological hooliganism;

I decided to dispose of the land and house, giving Chattunny Nair, the real estate prince of Khasak, the responsibility of selling them. The Papanasini would always flow in my mind in a covenant of everlasting memory.

A few days before I was to leave for Delhi, I had driven into town in my grandfather's Morris Minor to pick up whisky and sundry snacks. The phone rang when I was getting my favourite mini pakoras packed from KK Bakery. It was Amina calling from London; she was coming to Khasak to see her mother and would I fetch her from the airport? I assured her I would be glad to; I missed her. I had visited her mother just the day before; she seemed fine to me—chain-smoking beedis and drinking sweet milky tea. 'That girl worries too much; she should be thinking of work, not an old woman like me,' she complained.

When I told Amina her mother was fine, she muttered a grim 'Aha', which was never a good sign.

Amina and I had been lovers for a while, holidays in places like Siena and Shimla off and on. Neither of us being overly sentimental, and realising a good relationship was stronger than a mere love affair, we became good friends. I had WhatsApped her about my mother's death and she replied she wished she was there. Me too.

I collected her from Coimbatore airport; Amina looked and smelt good as always. She had grown her kohl-black hair long; I spotted a couple of white hairs. She smiled ruefully, having discerned my thoughts.

'White hair gets bankers taken seriously, especially if you're a woman,' she laughed. 'Why are you driving this contraption? No Bimmers in Kerala you could find?'

I was affronted. The Morris was family. The last remaining survivor of the line.

'Sentiment is a bad shock absorber,' she continued. 'Can't you drive any faster?'

'It doesn't go any faster,' I protested. 'And what's the hurry? Your mother is fine. Let's grab a beer.'

'Not a chance. I took a flight in the middle of an important merger to come here. My mother isn't fine.'

'She looks okay.'

'Looks aren't everything,' she muttered grimly. Amina wouldn't tell me more. I sensed she was deeply troubled and left her alone with her thoughts. We drove to her house in uneasy silence. Not letting me take her valise from the car's trunk, she asked me to meet her tomorrow. I didn't ask what was going on; besides, the real estate prince Chathunni Nair was bringing someone to see the house in the evening. I thought the discussion was promising.

I woke to a hangover and a phone call from Amina. I winced at the morning light coming through the windows, I had forgotten to draw the curtains. She ordered me to reach her mother's place 'pronto'. Having showered, bathed and stuffed my mouth with some cereal I drove off in the Morris Minor. When I reached, there were three people on the front yard. Amina, with her hands planted firmly at her waist, a thundercloud on her brow. Her mother in a white long-sleeved blouse and red checked lungi, sitting on her haunches and smoking a beedi. The motor mechanic Valsan, with studied nonchalance, was looking at a goat trying to climb the bamboo fence to eat adavippala leaves, his frizzy white hair and toothbrush moustache giving him the look of a Malayali Einstein. His eyes lit up at the sight of the Morris. He took a step forward when a sharp reprimand from Amina stopped him in his tracks.

'What's going on?' I pushed open the bamboo gate, and entered the compound. It was paved with cow dung, as it had been for decades. A mango tree in the corner scented the air. A regiment of ants was making its way in a disciplined line up the tree trunk, perhaps to dine on sweet mango gum. Everything was as it had been thirty years ago—pale yellow walls, curtainless windows, heavy iron-studded wooden planks nailed down to make a door and a low verandah with red oxide flooring. Only the working bulls and the oil wheel were gone.

'Well, go on, tell him,' Amina told her mother sternly.

The old lady had spruced herself up since the last time I saw her. Kajal in her eyes. Hair dyed black. Wrinkled face powdered. Her clothes, though old, were freshly laundered and ironed. She blew out a plume of beedi smoke in the air. Amina coughed.

'Tell me what?' I asked, confused.

'The thing is, kochumothalali, Amina mol is angry with us,' Valsan said feebly.

'Did I ask you? Don't you dare to call me mol. I'm not your daughter.'

'But you will be,' Amina's mother rose and went up to Valsan. She linked her arm in his, looked straight into my eyes and smiled widely. 'Valsan and I are getting married,' she announced.

Amina took a threatening step forward. Her mother raised her hand.

'I'm old and lonely, mole. Valsan is a good man. You're so far away, you can't always look after me. And I've no desire to live in the land of white people. When I caught pneumonia last year, you weren't around. When I slipped and fell in the backyard it was Valsan who took me to the hospital. He even cooked for me. I'm not blaming you, it is what it is.'

Amina opened her mouth and shut it. She looked both furious and guilty, if such a thing was possible.

'You children are so irresponsible you can't even think about how you'll be spending your old age,' She looked at me and Amina meaningfully.

'How did you know ...'

She silenced Amina with a wave of her hand. 'I know you better than you know yourself. I'm sure you're the one who broke it off.'

'How dare you?' Amina found her voice. I protested, telling the old lady that long-distance relationships don't last.

She grunted and said, 'We're getting married, Valsan and I, at Manapullikavu tomorrow at seven in the morning whether you like it or not. I called you in London to tell you that. I'll be happy if you come. If both of you come, or else ...' she shrugged.

'Over my dead body,' Amina snapped.

'It'll be my own dead body one of these days, Amina,' her mother said. 'Before that happens, I have a right to happiness. I had many suitors after your father died, but I refused them all because I didn't want you to feel bad or insecure. I didn't want you to be a stepdaughter, especially if I bore more children. I worked hard, selling gingelly oil and groceries to raise money for your education. I had no time for myself. And It's been years now since you left. I'm old and haven't had anybody for myself. I deserve that somebody.'

Valsan was almost in tears. He draped his hand over her shoulders.

'She's right. Come, get your things.' I took Amina's hand. 'You can sleep over at my place before it's sold.'

Amina broke into tears and buried her face in my chest. I patted her head gently. 'Come, let's go.' She nodded and went inside to pack.

'How's she behaving?' Valsan fondly chucked his chin at the Morris.

'You've kept her running like a race horse, thank you.'

He went to the car, stroked its bonnet lovingly and cooed to it.

The Morris took me and Amina home. I showed her into the guest room. She threw her bag on the bed. She walked in circles around the room, smoking furiously and dabbing her cheeks with my handkerchief that got progressively wetter.

'Is she right?' she stopped and asked me.

'What is right?' I gently sat her down on the bed.

'That we can't have relationships?'

'We've other things that make us happy.' I shrugged.

'Like what? One-night stands? Cocktail parties? Making partner? Buying a boat?'

'It isn't what is best in life that matters, but what is best for us, and that only we know. Maybe not now, but one day.'

'And what is best for you?'

'You were. For a while.'

'The same for me.'

'Well, there you go. We had each other in a way we never had anyone else, and we have a different each other now in a way nobody has. That works?'

'That works.' She flung her arms around my neck and kissed me on my cheek. Her wet mascara rubbed off on my face, and she laughed and wiped it away.

'Get out now, I want to think,' she shooed me out.

'Dinner?' I asked. She shut the door in my face.

I was woken up by loud banging on the door. It was dark outside; the night was being gently diluted by dawn. I cursed and padded over to the door and opened it. I gasped—for an insane moment I thought my mother stood there. It was Amina. She wore one of my mother's favorite kasavu saris. She had also managed to stick some jasmine flowers in her short hair.

'I hope you don't mind me borrowing auntie's sari.'

I nodded dumbly. Things were moving too fast for me.

'Let's be off. Go shower and get dressed,' she commanded.

'Off where?'

'To my mother's wedding, you jackass.' She came into my room to rummage in my wardrobe. She pulled out clothes, most of which she flung on my bed, until she settled on a white shirt and a Puliyilakaramundu. We made it to the temple in the nick of time, just when the couple had picked up the garlands. Valsan beamed widely when he saw us. Amina hugged her mother, sobbing uncontrollably. Her mother had tears in her eyes; she winked at me.

Amina accompanied the newlyweds out of the temple. I stayed back for a bit, to pray to the devi for their happiness, and for Amina's too. I did a proper namaskar. The priest blessed me with a sandalwood mark and a hibiscus. Amina, Valsan and his bride were waiting outside. They looked good together: a family of rich hearts.

'Let's go to the Indian Coffee House for breakfast, provided the food is as good as it was when I was a kid,' I suggested. Valsan assured me it was.

'What wedding present should we give them?' Amina asked.

It came to me in a flash; I knew exactly what to give them. Amina looked at me, and I knew the same thought had passed through her mind. I gave the keys of the Morris Minor to Valsan. 'Here is your wedding present. You've looked after her so well all these years that she deserves to be yours.'

Valsan broke into tears.

The couple dropped us off at Coimbatore airport; they were off to Ooty for their honeymoon. 'Make sure the old lady doesn't have a heart attack on the way up,' Amina said and giggled when her mother frowned, 'Not you, Mother, but the car.'

Valsan laughed and drove away, waving at us. We stood hand in hand watching them leave. Amina discreetly brushed a tear away.

Back in Delhi, I was certain I needed some recreation. Chathunni Nair had managed to get me an unexpectedly good price for the property. It had been quite a hectic trip, and emotional, but it had ended better than I could ever have imagined. I deserved a celebration. I preferred the girl friend experience to girlfriends; both cost money, but girlfriends invariably want to marry you, control you and produce noisy brats. Not that Amina was like that, but I haven't found anyone else who matched up to her fierce loyalty, her no-nonsense romanticism and weird sense of humour. I have a feeling she felt the same about me. But our single existence was more rewarding since it more or less allowed us to do anything we wished, or nothing at all for that matter. So, when I was lying in bed smoking a cigar and balancing a glass of a thirty-year-old whisky on a pretty navel after a pleasurable hour or two, and my iPad pinged, I cursed. Since it could be a client who wanted some quick work done and would pay in dollars, I padded over to my desk and logged in. I was glad I did. It was from my school friend in Dehradun, asking me to call. He is one of the few gentlemen of leisure left in that dreadful city—the son of a judge who had made piles of money by passing dubious verdicts exonerating British ne'er-do-wells and bought a magnificent colonial mansion in Clement Town. It had a garden with wrought iron benches where one could sit with a book in hand, sipping a Bloody Mary, before dozing off till the evening came around. My friend lives according to the vagaries of the weather: going on a bird shoot in Saharanpur or an illegal deer hunt in the forest reserve near Nahan in early winter. But most of all, he loves driving with the true passion of the dilettante racer, on roads that keep changing in his winding memories.

'Hey, I bought a Range Rover,' he told me over the phone after the usual insults traded between close friends were over. 'Lots of weddings and parties happening all around and it's time to drink and pig out. Remember our old schoolmate, the prince of Kashipur? He is getting married again and has invited me. I told him I'm bringing you.'

Prince of Kashipur indeed! If he is a prince, I'm Jawaharlal Nehru.

I recalled him as a snot-nosed boy with airs, who was regularly picked up on weekends in a Rolls Royce that had seen better times. He lived in a rambling old pile beside the Song River, to which he had once invited us for a surprisingly pleasant weekend.

'What say you?' My friend's voice sounded uncharacteristically tinny.

I felt a mild disquiet: he was famous in school as the choir boy with the loudest voice. Maybe it was the distance. Or he could have been hungover.

Was that chatter in the background? The monsoon, of course.

I thought he hated driving in the rain. Maybe the Range Rover had changed his perspective. Many years ago, when we had finished college and I was visiting him for a long weekend, we went on a long drive in his father's Ambassador, a relic from a leisurely age that will never return. It was a sturdy beast, bulky like an overgrown school bully. The gear shaft below the steering wheel was a tough lift and the engine a grumbling menace. The car's bonnet would begin to quiver when the speedometer neared sixty. Its shaft would rumble ominously when the wheels faltered over uneven roads. It took a wrestler's grip to open the little, triangular side glasses with their tiny comma-shaped handles. My friend hated driving in the rain. Getting the carburetor wet was his main fear; once we got stuck between Roorkee and Mohand at sunset and spent the night in the wilderness drinking whisky with rainwater, stretching out on the rexine-covered seats (no bucket seats then) and drifting off into inebriated sleep. The big car was a reassuring cocoon; it wasn't so bad getting stuck, we agreed later, just another driving adventure.

'I'll be there next weekend, how's that?' I asked on the phone.

He whooped. But something was missing—he didn't sound as hearty as usual. I was concerned. I asked him if he was okay.

'Better than the best-oiled Winchester 70. Downed a nilgai the other day with a single shot from seven hundred yards.'

'Bullshit.'

He laughed again, coughed and cleared his throat. 'This damn rain has given me a cold,' he explained.

'How's the old lady?' I asked.

'In the garage,' he said. 'I take her out for an airing now and then.'

'You want to show off your new Range Rover, huh?' I asked.

'Not really. But I just want to hang with you. Go for a drive in the rain. Get drunk. Talk of old times.'

The Range Rover would be very comfortable, I thought, its gears shifting silently and smoothly, power windows keeping out the complex smells of the rain-wet streets, the perfect suspension taking potholes with contempt, while its computers calibrated each gradient and curve. No more chunky gearshifts, no more monsoon breakdowns.

No romance either.

'Let's take the Ambassador,' I said.

Royal Flush

I had mail. It was from my friend in Landour. I hoped he wasn't inviting me to an illegal bird shoot; the fear of forest rangers gives me dyspepsia. After his father, an avid shooter, passed away a few years ago, leaving him pots of money and the large estate, he didn't have much to do but drink, read mysteries and hunt. His wife had divorced him; he didn't remarry. There is no sad tale here, he was a loner and had no use for female support.

The email was not about shooting. He had written, 'The old chap wants to win back the money he lost when we played poker twenty years ago at the Savoy. Come immediately.'

The old chap was our mutual friend who lived in Clement Town; the last I saw him was a couple of years ago when we went for a drive in his old car. It was a strange email, summoning someone from Kerala to travel more than 2,500 km for a game of cards. I asked why I had to drop everything and go over to play cards. 'Drop everything and come here to play cards,' was the answer. So I dropped everything and went, changing planes and taking a taxi from Jolly Grant airport for the last leg uphill to Landour. The vehicle groaned up the steep road through the bazaar to Mullingar and then with much protest took the zigzag incline to Landour. I passed St Paul's Church where the records of the 1857 Mutiny are still stored, and Chaar Dukaan—there were at least six shops there by now—where noisy tourists in loud clothes and glue-stuck honeymooners from the plains wolfed down oily parathas and Maggi noodles. Landour used to be a quiet place of cedars and cemeteries.

I was keen to see my school friends again. They were sitting on the porch of the house, watching the golden light reluctantly retreating over the manicured lawn towards the deodars. I paid off the taxi. The house help came to take my bags. My host gave me a huge hug. His eyes seemed suspiciously wet. My other friend smiled and waved from his chair. I asked him why he was being such a hotshot and not giving me a hug when I realised he was in a wheelchair. Even when we were young, we were never sentimental. Didn't seem right somehow. This time, my heart clenched.

'Copying Morgan Freeman in *The Bucket List?*' I joked weakly. He laughed, and in the middle of it choked up. We thumped his back and patted his head. He drew a shallow breath and spat out a blob of blood and phlegm.

'I'm better looking than Freeman,' he shot back.

He had a rasping cough, which got worse when he talked. He would take little breaks and pull his oxygen mask over his face and take deep breaths.

'Look at us, the Three Musketeers. Forty-five years later nothing has changed,' he gurgled from behind the mask and stretched out his hand to shake mine. His grip was powerful, like a wrestler's.

'It's his lungs,' our host said morosely. 'I thought friends had warranties.'

'Warranties expire, you know.' That cough again. More blood. 'I was waiting for you,' he turned to me. 'I have to get my money back. We play tonight, okay?' He was still sore about me beating his hand at poker with a royal flush years ago.

We carried him in his wheelchair to the car; he was as light as thistledown. We drove to the Savoy at the other end of Mussoorie, braving the clumsy SUVs and eluding the clusters of motorcyclists and overloaded tourist buses clogging the traffic circle at the Mall Road intersection. I was visiting the Savoy after decades; it seemed different, impersonal. It had personality, having been built by an Irish barrister in 1902. It was the only hotel in British India to have its own post office. It was a ruin when I last dropped in at the turn of the century to drink in the Writer's Bar with my two buddies. A waiter, possibly as old as the hotel itself, had served us salted peanuts and soggy potato wedges. We spotted Mussoorie's resident writer Ruskin Bond with his longtime friend Ganesh Saili.

'Come to show your friends the ghosts?' Ganesh called out to his fellow Landourian.

The Savoy has a reputation for ghosts who haven't checked out for centuries: the spectre of Lady Garnet who was poisoned to death walks the corridors, and a cloaked figure pops up in the hotel's vestibule only to slowly disappear into the shadows of the musty lounge. To me, it looked like any other pimped-up heritage hotel confused about the century it belongs to. The walls still sported vintage photographs of Nehru, Indira Gandhi, Mountbatten, kings and queens, tiger hunts and Hollywood actresses. But there were unpleasant intrusions into history—photos of a bald man with oily pomaded hair and tacky tailoring receiving an award from some local politician and parading around with various indigenous VIPs. The hotel that had inspired Agatha Christie to write *The Mysterious Affair at Styles* now had as much style as a hustler wearing a pawnshop tuxedo.

'Not here,' my friend said mournfully from his wheelchair, adjusting the tartan blanket covering his legs. 'I can't play poker here.'

He didn't have to. Our host had the foresight to book a room with atmosphere. Mussoorie's old Savoyphiles say the room is haunted by a certain McClintock's ghost who played the piano. The piano was sold off long ago, although legend says you can still hear McClintock tickle the ivories: an invisible ghost playing an invisible piano. The spirit of the Savoy could not be wiped away just like that by any nouveau riche hotelier.

A card table had been placed by the window. The heater had been turned up, making the room comfortably warm to ward off any chill McClintock's ghost would send our way. A side table was set up with three crystal glasses and a bottle of Scotch of excellent vintage.

'Who deals first?' came the question from the wheelchair.

'If you tell us a Sufi story we've never heard before, you can go first,' our host offered.

'Deal,' he said, and almost died coughing. His Sufi stories were legendary in college and he would seduce the best looking girls, including the English teacher, with his mystical humour. 'Women can't resist spirituality with a dash of fun, that's my secret,' he would boast.

This time, he told us a Sufi story about playing cards. We drank, laughed and cheated, spoke of old times, and played rummy until I saw the dawn breaking with a pink blush.

'Your hand, buddy,' I yawned.

My friend didn't move from his wheelchair. His head was tilted to one side. A hand of cards was held loosely in his lap.

'Must be tired and dozed off,' out host ventured hopefully.

I checked his pulse and shook my head. 'What a strange way to bid adieu.'

'Let's see his hand.' My friend picked up the cards. It was a royal flush.

'At least he won the game,' said the host.

'The bastard probably cheated,' I laughed and began to cry.

People speak about processing grief. But you cannot process grief; it is not tinned cheese or a Cola. You can only live it one day at a time, hour by hour, until the emptiness loses its sharp edges and becomes a part of everything you do. It becomes the cold in the breeze, the ivory in the piano, the orange in the flames of the fireplace. It is the guest who will not leave until its deadly sibling comes calling.

I could have stayed back in Landour for a few days, sharing stories about our departed friend whose farewell was a card game. I could have gone on long walks with my host along the curving roads of the hill station, as we used to when there were three of us, invading the cemetery at night and probably scaring off the specters of seventeenth-century Englishmen.

I realised my host was feeling lonely for the first time in his life since he met us. Our eyes locked across the roof of the taxi that was taking me to the airport. Like we always could, we read the thought that passed through our minds simultaneously. 'Who'll be the last one left?'

I'm being selfish, I know, but I hope it will not be me. There are no more goodbyes left in me.

My Friend
the Sufi

Sacrilege

A Sufi was passing by a temple when he saw the imam hitting a dog.

'Wait, what has he done?' he asked.

'This wretched animal has committed sacrilege. It entered the sanctum sanctorum and ate all the offerings.'

'Did the dog know it was committing sacrilege?'

'Of course not. It's just a stupid dog.'

'Does God know it was committing sacrilege?'

'What a stupid question. How do I know?'

'God knows,' said the Sufi, and walked away with the dog.

Enlightenment

A boy asked the Sufi to teach him enlightenment.

The Sufi pointed to a red rose bush and asked the boy to bring him one. The boy did as instructed. The Sufi muttered a few words and made some magical gestures. The rose turned white.

The boy clapped his hands and exclaimed, 'You're truly enlightened, Master. Teach me how to do that.'

'If I was enlightened, would I be sitting here changing the colour of roses for a silly boy like you?' the Sufi said.

The Loan

The Sufi went to the local moneylender for a loan to buy himself a new robe and a darbuka.

'I can't give you money. You are a man of God with no possessions. How will you pay me back?'

'God will pay you back.'

'God is not my debtor.'

'No, but you are His.'

A Fair Trade

The Sufi went to the market to buy a horse.

'What kind of horse are you looking for?' a wily trader asked him.

'I don't know anything about horses. Any fine one will do.'

The trader showed him a donkey, claiming it was the best horse he had, and he was offering it cheap because he respected God. They haggled over the price and finally settled on twenty rupees.

The Sufi looked around and chose twenty pebbles from the ground. He gave these to the trader.

'What! This isn't money, you're giving me pebbles for a horse?'

'That's how much a donkey costs disguised as a horse,' the Sufi said, and rode away.

Silence

The Sufi was sitting in the middle of a crowded market with his eyes closed. The atheist stopped and laughed contemptuously. 'Foolish man, how can you mediate in such a noisy place?' he asked.

'I'm not meditating. I'm listening to the sound of silence.'

'Silence? Just listen to that din! I'm almost going deaf.'

'Can't you hear the silence hiding between the sounds?'

'You're crazy. How can anyone hear silence in noise?'

'If you shut up, I will show you,' said the Sufi, and closed his eyes.

Perspective

The Sufi was standing on his head in the middle of the road. The atheist asked him what he was doing.

'I'm looking at you. Why are you upside down?'

Hearing the exchange, an amused crowd collected at the spot.

The atheist laughed at the Sufi. 'You're the one seeing the world upside down.'

'It is a matter of perspective,' the Sufi said, getting up.

He stretched and looked around, then said, 'Ah, now we are all upside down.'

Skill Development

The Sufi was wandering in the village bazaar when he came across a man with a monkey on his shoulder. The Sufi asked him if the animal was well trained.

'I can train anything, even your God,' boasted the owner.

The Sufi gave the monkey a tight slap. The monkey, as was its nature, imitated the Sufi and slapped its master in turn.

'What did you just do?' the outraged trainer asked.

'I didn't do anything, it was the monkey that slapped you. If you can't even train a monkey, how will you train God?'

Making the Point

The Sufi was pruning the branches of a dead tree outside the mosque. It had been around forever and nobody had the heart to cut it down.

'Don't you know it's a dead tree?' asked the atheist.

'Why do you ask me trick questions you know I will answer?'

'Is that your answer or a question?'

The Sufi handed his shears to the atheist and got down from the ladder.

'I'm going for lunch at the bazaar. You can prune these.'

'What is the point of giving me this pointless task?'

'Unless you can tell when a task is pointless, how will you know which task has a point?' asked the Sufi, and went off to his favourite inn to order wine and bread.

The Art of Listening

The Sufi was smoking his hookah under the banyan tree when a young man walked by.

'Hey, I haven't seen you for a few years. You told me you were going to the mountains to seek answers.'

'I've finally given up,' the man said. 'He never answers me.'

'What do you say to Him?' asked the Sufi.

'I ask for strength, peace, clarity,'

'And what do you get?'

'Silence.'

The Sufi shrugged. 'It's not enough to ask, you have to know when you are answered.'

What's the Use?

The Sufi was whispering into the ear of a goat when the atheist passed by.

'She broke into my neighbour's godown and ate all the bananas. I'm speaking to his soul, telling him that thieving is bad, even for a goat.'

'You are wasting your time, old man. Goats have no soul.'

The goat bleated.

'See?' said the Sufi. 'He disagrees.'

'That's just noise.'

'So is most philosophy,' said the Sufi. 'But at least the goat gives milk.'

Looking for God

The Sufi was sitting on a charpoi when the atheist came by.
    'What are you doing here?' the atheist asked.
    'Looking for God, as usual,' said the Sufi.
    "How will you recognise him?
    'I didn't say I'd found Him. Only that I'm looking.'
    'But you've looked for years!'
    'And you've doubted for years. Neither of us has changed much.'
    'At least I'm honest about it.'
    'So am I. I'm looking for something I can't describe.'
    The atheist crossed his arms. 'And if you never find Him?'
    The Sufi smiled. 'Then at least I won't have spent my life talking to myself.'

The Image of God

The Sufi heard that the king was offering a reward of ten gold coins for the artist who made the most beautiful image of God. He approached his friend, the sculptor, and asked him to make a bust in his likeness.

On the appointed day, he took it to the king and claimed his reward.

'You dare mock me?' The king was furious. 'Does this mean you consider yourself God?'

'God is everyone and everything. He is you, me and them. So I got an image made of the God I know.'

The king understood. He ordered that the bust be displayed prominently in the palace, gave the Sufi an extra ten gold coins, and sent him on his way.

God's Pleasures

Alarmed that young people were straying from God's path, the imam imposed a ban on drinking, dancing and visiting pleasure houses.

One day, he saw the Sufi counting prayer beads outside the mosque.

'I'm praying for death,' the Sufi told the imam.

'What a strange man you are. Who prays for his own death?'

'When all pleasure is killed in God's name, it's a pleasure to die in God's name,' the Sufi replied.

'Pleasures are the devil's work,' cried the imam.

'Everything is God's work; the devil, too,' said the Sufi.

The imam, enlightened, lifted the ban, and young people visited the mosque more frequently to thank God for their happiness.

Biryani at a Funeral

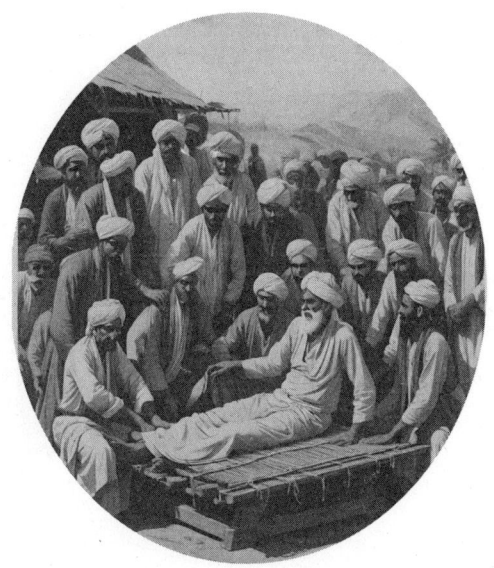

The Sufi invited the village to his funeral the following day.

'Will there be biryani?' asked the atheist.

'Yes,' said the Sufi. 'But only if I'm satisfied with the rehearsal.'

'What rehearsal?'

The next morning, mourners arrived. Verses were read. Biryani was served. Halfway through lunch, the Sufi sat up and ate a spoonful. 'Too much cardamom,' he scolded. 'And the rice is undercooked.'

The atheist was surprised, 'You said you were dead!'

'I said I'd die,' said the Sufi. 'I never said I'd stay that way.'

'But why go through all this?' cried the imam.

'I want to enjoy my funeral while I can still taste the food.'

Heirloom

A woman was carrying a beautifully painted earthen pot of milk to the temple when she tripped and fell. The pot broke into pieces.

She began to wail at her misfortune. The Sufi, who was passing by, stopped to inquire.

'My mother gave me this pot to take milk to the temple and offer it to God. Now what shall I do?' she sobbed.

'Get another pot, many like this are available,' the Sufi suggested.

'This one was an heirloom. It cannot be replaced.'

'Go to the market and buy another pot just like this one. Give it to your son. It will become his heirloom if he loves you as much as you loved your mother,' advised the Sufi.

Enjoyment

The Sufi was inspecting a melon in the market when the atheist came by. 'Are you checking to see if God has ripened it?' he asked sarcastically.

'Can you tell when a melon becomes ripe?' The Sufi showed the atheist the fruit.

'I don't know anything about melons, ask your God,' the atheist sneered.

'I was checking whether you know what God knows.'

'All I know is there is no God,' the atheist laughed.

'Now there is no melon either,' the Sufi said. He smashed the fruit on the atheist's head and walked away whistling.

Boredom

The atheist was passing by the village pond when he saw the Sufi sitting by its edge and staring into the water.

'What are you doing?' the atheist asked.

'What I was doing yesterday. And what I'll be doing tomorrow,' the Sufi replied.

'What are you looking at?'

'My reflection.'

'Aren't you bored?'

'Yes, but my reflection isn't.'

Sun on Sale

In the village market the Sufi saw a trickster trying to sell the sun to a peasant who was returning from the bazaar with a large sum of money. 'You can sell sunlight to everyone and become a milionaire,' the crook said, showing the peasant a scroll. It stated he owned the sun, which he was entitled to sell to anyone for ten silver coins.

'Wait, is this really the ownership deed of the sun?' the Sufi asked.

The trickster nodded.

The Sufi took the scroll and tore it into two.

'What have you done?' the con man screamed at the Sufi.

'The sun just set,' said the Sufi, throwing the paper to the ground.

SEEING

A Sufi was watering an empty flower pot.

A gardener stopped, puzzled by the Sufi's behaviour. 'Why are you watering an empty pot?' he asked.

'I don't see an empty pot, I can only see the plant,' the Sufi replied.

'You're mad. There's no plant in this, it's an empty pot.'

'If you can't see the plant in an empty pot, how will you grow your garden?' asked the Sufi, and walked way laughing.

The Devil in Disguise

The atheist came to where the Sufi was chatting with villagers in the mosque.

'Sufi, I'm troubled. I dreamt of God last night,' he said.

'Aha. So you admit there is god. What did he look like?'

'This is no time to joke, Sufi. God has horns, pointed teeth, big bloody claws and a cloven foot. His tail ends in an arrow.'

'You dreamt of the devil, you fool,' laughed one of the villagers.

'Remember God comes in all forms,' the Sufi interrupted. 'This time he came disguised as the devil with whom this gentleman has a longstanding relationship.'

ACKNOWLEDGEMENTS

My deepest gratitude and love to my childhood hero and grandfather Ooottupilakkal Velukutty who is an integral part of this book, my grandmother Thachamoochikkal Kamalakshi, my great grandmother Kalyani and my parents Santha and Etteth Gangadharan, without whose stories this book wouldn't have happened. I express my profound admiration for my great grandfather Chamiyachan, who played an important part in the temple entry agitation but ended up as a footnote in the history of Malabar. To Ramaswamy, for all those days and nights of companionship in my childhood. My heartfelt thanks to my childhood friend Sheila Kumar for correcting me on all Palakkad-related facts. My gratitude to Sapna Kapoor for applying her design talent and, a big thank you to Vivan Kamath for finessing the cover with better detailing. Above all, many thanks to my long-suffering editor V.K. Karthika, who deserves both my loyalty and love for putting up with my vacillations with patience.